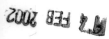

..., she
llowed
every
e was
ifficult
und in
ends a
a place
plot of
he was
in the
ying to

DG 02242/71

there is
n't ring
true.

Anthony Masters, TES

BALLOON HOUSE

ORCHARD BOOKS
96 Leonard Street, London EC2A 4XD
Orchard Books Australia
14 Mars Road, Lane Cove, NSW 2066
First published in Great Britain in 2000
Paperback original
Text © Brian Keaney, 2000
The right of Brian Keaney to be identified as the
author of this work has been asserted by him
in accordance with the Copyright,
Designs and Patents Act, 1988.
A CIP catalogue record for this book is
available from the British Library.
1 84121 437 X
3 5 7 9 10 8 6 4 2
Printed in Great Britain

BRIAN KEANEY

BALLOON HOUSE

ORCHARD BOOKS

CHAPTER ONE

Once upon a time there was a Great Magician and he lived in a house called Balloon House. On the top of this house the Great Magician had fitted an enormous balloon so that whenever he got tired of where he was living he would pull on a lever and, with a hissing of air, the enormous balloon would start to inflate. First the house would begin to wobble, then it would begin to shake, until finally it lifted off the ground entirely and floated away through the air.

It seemed to Neve that winter was lasting for ever. It was the middle of February and every day the sky over London was the same dull shade of grey. It didn't matter that the trees in her street were beginning to show tiny pink blossoms, spring was still an impossibly long time away. Every year at this time those trees blossomed hopefully while the city was still firmly held in the grip of winter and every year the wind and the rain tore the blossoms from the branches within a couple of weeks. Neve had no idea what kind of trees they were but she suspected that they were meant to bloom in a different climate, one in which February was not iron-cold, slate-grey and pierced by a bitter wind.

She sat on the sofa in the front room of her house, looking out through the net-curtained window at the traffic that went past. The street on which she lived reminded her at times of a river. The houses stood on the banks on either side. Down the middle flowed an endless current of cars which never really stopped even in the small hours of the night. An hour ago it had been rush hour and that river had been in full flood as returning workers had surged past bumper-to-bumper in their cars. Now the flow was slackening but it would be a long time yet before it had slowed down to a trickle.

Apart from summer holidays spent in Brittany and a school trip to Cologne, London was all that Neve had ever known. Sometimes she wondered what it would be like to sit in her front room and look out on a different landscape, one in which there were mountains, green fields or even a real river, not just an endless stream of traffic. She imagined stepping out of the front door and breathing in the fresh smell of pine needles and rain-soaked earth instead of petrol fumes. But that was just a dream. This was the reality.

Ordinarily she did not mind living in London. It was the world she had been born into, the only one she knew, and most of the time she was quite content with it. But not today. Today she was not content with anything. She had been feeling fidgety all day long. It was because of Laurence, of course. It annoyed her to think that her father could turn her world upside down so easily but there was nothing she could do about it. In a few minutes he would stop his car outside the house, get out and ring the doorbell. She wondered what he would say when he saw her and whether he would look any different, older probably. She wondered if he would have picked up a French accent. Most of all she wondered about Yvonne.

Yvonne was her father's new wife. It sounded really strange put like that. He had met her in Paris not very long after he had been posted there by the newspaper for which he worked. It had been a whirlwind romance. They had got married just eight weeks after their first meeting. That was typical of her father. He didn't believe in letting the grass grow under his feet.

Yvonne worked as a translator. She spoke several different languages, or so Laurence had said in one of his letters. That must be really satisfying, Neve thought, to be able to go to different countries and speak to the people in their own languages. She could not imagine herself ever being able to do such a thing. In her mind she had already formed a picture of Yvonne. She imagined her as slim, chic, very fashionably dressed, her dark hair cut short, perhaps in a bob. She saw Yvonne walking along a street in Paris, going into a café and ordering coffee in an impeccable French accent. She saw her sitting down at a table, opening a French newspaper and beginning to read.

Neve got up from the sofa, went out of the front room and up the stairs to her bedroom. She stood in front of the mirror and looked at herself. Her hair was a mess. She had been wearing it short for years. Then a few months ago she had decided to grow it. Now it was at an in-between stage which looked dreadful. She tried pulling it back in a ponytail but that was no improvement. It was too severe. She let it go again. It would just have to look messy. There was nothing she could do about it.

She had already spent ages trying to decide what to wear. She could not make up her mind whether she should get dressed up or not. She had asked her mother. 'It's up to you,' her mother had said, not very helpfully. Then she had added. 'I should wear something you feel comfortable in.'

It was not as if Neve had never been for a meal in a restaurant before. It was just that there were so many things she wasn't sure about. For a start, she didn't know whether or not this was going to be a really expensive restaurant. She didn't want to be the only person there who wasn't smartly dressed. On the other hand she didn't want to overdo it either. Actually she didn't really feel like going at all. Of course she wanted to see her dad but she wished that their first meeting in two years could have taken place somewhere a little less public and she especially wished that Yvonne didn't have to be there. But Yvonne was part of the package these days. There was no escaping her.

Maybe she should put on something just a little bit smarter, she decided. After all, you could never predict what her father would do. She wouldn't put it past him to take her to the most expensive restaurant in London. She started taking clothes out of her wardrobe and putting them on the bed. The trouble was she didn't really have any smart clothes, well none that she liked at any rate. Everything that she took out of the wardrobe seemed to have something wrong with it. She held up a blue dress that she had bought a few months earlier. Then she imagined it under Yvonne's sophisticated glance. She put it down again.

'Are you all right in there?' her mother asked, poking her head round the door. 'You're not still trying to decide what to wear, surely?'

'I wish I wasn't going,' Neve told her.

'Don't be silly. You don't mean that,' her mother said. But Neve did. Right then she was wishing she could just call the whole thing off.

'Let me look at you,' her mother said. She surveyed Neve critically. 'You look fine.'

'Are you sure?'

'I'm certain.'

'But am I smart enough?'

'Perfectly.'

Neve sat down on the bed and her mother sat down beside her. 'What's the matter?' her mother asked.

Neve sighed. 'I hate the way...' she began. Then she stopped.

'You hate the way what?'

'Oh nothing.' Neve had been going to say that she hated the way her father could just disappear out of her life completely and then reappear two years later and expect everything to be just fine. But she knew there was no point in saying that to her mother. Judith was far too fair-minded to look at things in that way.

However, her mother must have known what she was thinking. 'It probably won't be easy for anyone,' she said.

'I wish you were coming,' Neve replied, then immediately she regretted it. Of course her mother couldn't come. That would have been asking too much. Judith would not have wanted to sit across the table from her ex-husband and his new wife and make small talk about the weather in England or the food in Paris. She wondered what her mother felt about her father now but she could not come right out and ask her.

Judith was a small person, physically. Just the other day when they had both been standing in the kitchen, Neve had realised that her mother was only a couple of centimetres taller than she was. She was small-boned and fine-featured and when she was younger she had been pretty. Nowadays the lines at the corners of her eyes were too deeply etched to describe her as still pretty but she could still look good if she wanted to. Despite her physical stature she was a strong person with a strength that seemed to come from inside, as if she was determined not to let the world push her around. As a result she could be quite intimidating, but only when she needed to be. Most of the time she was gentle and considerate to the feelings of others. Neve wished she could be more like her instead of indecisive, easily pushed around and then afterwards always regretting what had happened. Judith took her hand. 'Just try to enjoy the evening,' she told Neve. 'If I know your father the food will be really good.'

'I'm not hungry,' Neve said stubbornly.

'I expect you'll change your mind by the time you get to the restaurant.'

Just then the doorbell rang. 'There they are now,' her mother continued. She hesitated for a moment then she stood up. 'I'll answer,' she said.

In that second's delay it occurred to Neve that this evening was hard for her mother also, that she probably found it very difficult to go downstairs and open the door. She wondered who would be waiting on the other side. Would it be just her dad or would Yvonne be standing there with him? She picked up her coat, put it on hurriedly and went downstairs. Her mother was standing at the door talking to her father. There was no sign of Yvonne.

The first thing you noticed about Laurence was his eyes. They were a very pale blue and at this moment they were looking over Judith's shoulder directly at Neve. He was smiling broadly but there was a hint of anxiety about him too, as if he was not sure what kind of a reception to expect. 'Here she is!' he announced. 'Your carriage awaits you, madam.'

Her mother stood back to allow her to pass. 'Hello, Dad,' Neve said.

His fair hair was cut shorter than she remembered and he was wearing a long overcoat which emphasised how slim he was. He looked good for his age, Neve thought. For some reason that annoyed her. It was as if leaving his family behind had done him good.

'Is that all I get?' he said, 'after two years without seeing you. "Hello, Dad"!'

She leaned forward and kissed him on the cheek.

He put his arms around her and hugged her.

'You won't keep her out too late, will you?' Judith asked.

'Of course I won't,' Laurence said. He handed her a card. 'This is the number of the restaurant if you should need to contact us for any reason.' He turned back to Neve. 'Ready then?'

She nodded.

'Right. Let's go.'

'Well you've certainly changed,' her father told her.

'Have I? In what way?'

'You've grown about a metre.'

'Don't be ridiculous!' she said, but she smiled. It was what she wanted to hear.

'What happened to the little girl I left behind?'

'She grew up,' Neve told him. 'It's been two years, you know.' She tried to keep the note of accusation out of her voice, but it crept in despite her.

'I know,' her father said. 'But I'm back now. We'll be able to see a lot of each other from now on.' He stopped in front of a red car. 'Here we are.'

The woman who was sitting in the front passenger seat was not at all like Neve had imagined Yvonne to be. There was nothing very sophisticated about her.

In fact she was very ordinary looking. She opened the door when she caught sight of them and got out. She was dressed in beige trousers and a red twin-set and had shoulder-length blonde hair. 'Hi,' she said. 'I'm Yvonne.' She held out her hand.

'Hello,' Neve said. She took the hand that Yvonne offered and shook it.

'Shall I sit in the back?' Yvonne said. 'You two must have lots to say to each other.'

'It's all right,' Neve said. 'I'll get in the back.' She opened the door and got in. Yvonne got back into the front seat. Neve couldn't help noticing that she was a little bit overweight. She was certainly nothing like as good-looking as Judith, she decided, with satisfaction.

Her father got into the driver's seat. 'I hope you still like pasta,' he said.

'Yes, I do,' Neve told him. Despite her earlier insistence that she was not hungry, the thought of Italian food was suddenly tremendously attractive.

'You'll like this place,' her father said. 'It's not at all grand but the food is wonderful. We discovered it a fortnight ago after coming out of the theatre.'

Neve felt a little stab of jealousy when she heard this. She imagined her father coming out of a theatre hand in hand with Yvonne, talking about the play that they had seen, not thinking for a minute about the life he had abandoned.

'As soon as we sat down, I thought, Neve would like this restaurant,' he went on, immediately making Neve feel guilty for what she had just thought. 'That's one thing that you and Yvonne have in common,' he added. 'You're both fans of Italian cooking.'

Yvonne turned round in her seat to talk to Neve. 'Have you ever been to Italy?' she asked.

Neve shook her head.

'It's a beautiful country.'

'Do you speak Italian?' Neve asked.

'Yvonne speaks about fifty languages,' Laurence said.

'Do you really?'

'Of course not,' Yvonne replied, 'only French, Italian and a bit of Spanish. Your father is the most terrible liar.' She turned back to face him, smiling like a young girl who is being teased by her boyfriend. It was an attitude that Neve found slightly embarrassing.

'I'm not a liar,' her father said. 'I just like to colour the facts, that's all.'

'Typical journalist!' Yvonne said. It was intended

as a playful insult but Neve could tell that Yvonne really thought her father was marvellous. It was obvious just from the way that she looked at him that she thought everything he said was incredibly clever and amazingly witty.

'I'm a natural storyteller, that's all,' Laurence protested. 'Isn't that right, Neve?'

'Uh-huh,' Neve said. She didn't feel that he needed any more encouragement.

'So tell me all your news,' he went on. Her father always liked to talk when he drove. He was one of those people who could thread his way through three lanes of traffic while telling a joke at the same time, unlike her mother who always drove in silence giving her full concentration to the road ahead.

'What news?' Neve asked.

'I don't know,' her father said. 'Let me see, in the last letter I got from you, you were planning to decorate your bedroom.'

'That was ages ago,' Neve told him.

'Well maybe you should write more often,' her father said, jokingly.

Neve wasn't prepared to let him get away with that. 'Maybe you should come and see me more often,' she pointed out.

'Ouch!' her father said. 'That was a bit below the belt.'

'You asked for it.'

To Neve's annoyance, Yvonne reached across and rested her hand consolingly on Laurence's shoulder. Neve wanted to say, 'Don't do that. He deserved it.' But she said nothing.

'Well how did the decorating go, anyway?' he continued.

'OK. Mum did most of it. I only did the easy bits.'

'What colour did you choose?'

'Blue.'

'We've been decorating, too,' Yvonne said. 'Haven't we, Laurence?'

'We certainly have,' he said. 'You'll have to come and see our new house. It's a bit rough and ready at the moment but it's going to be terrific.'

'And you'll be able to meet Daniel,' Yvonne went on.

Daniel was Yvonne's and her father's baby. He had been born about three months before they left France. Her father had sent her a photograph with his last letter. It showed a tiny baby lying on a rug, one hand clutched to his chest, the other one held out in front of him in a fist as if he were a boxer. On the card he had written, '*Daniel is fighting fit.*' Most of that letter had been about Daniel and what a well-behaved baby he was. Neve had been faintly irritated that he assumed she would be so interested.

'I've told Daniel about you,' Yvonne said. 'I'm sure he's looking forward to meeting you.'

'What?' Neve said. 'But he's only a few months old.'

'It's important to talk to babies just as you would to adults,' Yvonne said. She sounded as if she were repeating something she had learned by heart.

'But what's the point if they can't understand?' Neve asked her.

'They understand a great deal more than people think,' Yvonne went on.

'Oh right! He's really going to understand about me, isn't he?' Neve said. 'Did you explain about divorce as well?'

There was silence in the car. Neve realised that she had gone too far. Yvonne was obviously offended. Well it was her own fault for being stupid.

'Look at the lights on the river,' her father said, changing the subject. Neve looked out of the window at the streetlamps reflecting in the murky waters of the Thames. 'People say Paris is beautiful,' he went on, 'but there's nowhere like London.' He carried on talking about the relative merits of different cities but Neve had stopped listening. She was studying Yvonne's double chin. It was not a really bad one, except when she bent her head forwards. No doubt that was what Daniel saw when Yvonne bent over him. She wondered whether Yvonne had thought about that. She knew that it wasn't very nice of her to think such things but it was enjoyable and, after all, that was what she was supposed to be doing, enjoying herself.

A gust of warm air hit them as they went through the glass doors of the restaurant. It was a welcome relief after the chilly walk through the network of little streets that led from the car park. Neve had expected somewhere small and dark with candles guttering in winebottles and elderly waiters with bow-ties and thick moustaches. But this was big and bright with marble walls and a tiled floor. It looked very new, almost gleaming. A young, good-looking waiter in a white, open-necked shirt and black waistcoat showed them to their table. He pulled back the chair for Neve to sit down, then left them to study the menu.

Neve looked about her. There were pieces of what looked like antique statues dotted about the restaurant. Beside their table was the stone head of a woman. She pointed it out to her father.

'Reproduction, I'm afraid,' he said. 'But wait till you taste the food. I guarantee that is the real thing.'

Now that Neve could see other people eating and smell their food, she realised that she was absolutely starving.

'What will you have for a starter?' her dad asked.

Neve stared at the list of starters with their exotic names and tempting descriptions. 'I can't decide,' she said.

'There's no hurry,' he told her.

'Do you know what you're having?' she asked.

He nodded. 'I'm having the goats' cheese salad.'

Neve made a face. She had tried goats' cheese before and had not enjoyed the experience.

'And I'm having the Gnocchi Modena to follow,' he continued.

'I'll have the same,' Yvonne said.

Neve had been about to say that she would have that but now that Yvonne had beaten her to it she felt that she must come up with her own choice. Annoyed, she studied the menu again. How could such a simple thing as choosing a meal be so very difficult?

'Making up her mind has never been Neve's strong point,' Laurence told Yvonne.

That made Neve angry. He was just trying to be funny at her expense. 'At least I make my own mind up,' she said. 'I don't copy other people.'

Yvonne raised her eyebrows but said nothing. Neve knew that she had probably gone too far again but she didn't care. In the end she chose minestrone soup for a starter followed by pizza. It wasn't a particularly adventurous choice but at least she knew what she was getting.

It was not turning out to be a particularly successful evening. Neve could see that. She realised that it was partly her fault. After all, she hadn't exactly been friendly. But her father and Yvonne were also to blame. They were too caught up in their own lives to really listen to anything that she had to say. Laurence asked her questions about her life, but the questions themselves showed how little he knew about her. 'Who *do* you like then nowadays?' he asked, after she had pointed out to him that his memory of the kind of music she enjoyed was at least two years out of date.

She mentioned the names of some of her favourite

pop groups. He shook his head. 'Never heard of them,' he said. 'What else do you like doing, apart from listening to music?'

'I can't just come up with a big list of things that I'm interested in,' Neve protested. 'No one can, not just like that.'

'I can,' he insisted. 'Let me see, I like good food.'

'I see what's number one on the list,' Yvonne said.

'I also appreciate the company of the people I am close to,' Laurence went on. 'I'm fond of good conversation, French wine, Italian food, Beethoven and modern jazz, I like...'

'The sound of your own voice,' Neve interrupted.

Laurence stopped abruptly. 'That put me in my place,' he said.

But he did not stay in his place for long. He was soon off again talking about the most beautiful and the most terrible sights that he had seen. The way he spoke about them made you want to listen, to hear more. He was right when he had described himself as a good storyteller. But all his stories that evening were about places that Neve had never been to.

After they had ordered their food, an elderly man and woman came into the restaurant. There was nothing special about them. He was bald, red-faced with a little moustache, a bit overweight but smartly dressed in a suit and tie. She was thin and rather worried-looking. She gave the impression of tagging along after him like a little dog. As soon as she caught sight of them, Yvonne stared. Then she nudged Laurence and said, in a whisper, 'Look it's the major-general and he's got his wife with him.' She seemed very pleased with what she had said, as if she had just made an incredibly amusing joke. Laurence glanced over at the new arrivals who were standing, looking around the restaurant, waiting for a waiter to show them to their table. Then he turned away again with a knowing smile. It was clear that he, too, found something incredibly funny about them.

He turned to Neve. 'In the office where I used to work in Paris,' he said, 'there was a man who was in charge of the reception desk on the night shift. We called him the major-general. The man who has just come in looks very like him.'

'Was he in the army?' Neve said, not really under-standing what was so funny.

'No. He just looked like he should have been.'

'And he acted like it, too,' Yvonne said. 'He was very fierce. He insisted on visitors signing in and out, even when he knew perfectly well who they were and what they were doing. He made it abundantly clear that he didn't think much of a young woman coming into the office late at night to wait for a man she wasn't married to.'

It was on the tip of Neve's tongue to ask who this young woman was that Yvonne was talking about. But then she realised that Yvonne meant herself. That was rather a flattering description, in Neve's opinion.

Laurence must have realised that he and Yvonne were sharing a private joke because he began again trying to include her in the conversation. 'So, how's school then?' he asked.

People only ever asked you how school was when they were absolutely desperate for something to talk about because it was completely impossible to describe school life. There was either nothing to say or far too much, depending on how you looked at it. You could go into extreme detail, describing all the teachers, their different personalities, the subjects they taught, the students they favoured and the ones they disliked. You could list assignments you had written, problems you had solved, marks you had got and comments that had been made. You could talk about your friends, their ideas about fashion and music, the quarrels they had with each other and with you and the reconciliations that had taken place. Alternatively you could just say, 'OK'. That was the course of action Neve opted for.

'Only OK?' her father said, disappointedly. 'I was hoping to hear that you were the school's star pupil.'

Neve shook her head. 'I'm afraid not.'

'I expect she's just being modest,' Yvonne said. 'With such a brilliant father she couldn't help being an outstanding student.'

Neve was filled with an urge to pick up the bottle of red wine that the waiter had brought a few minutes earlier and empty it all over Yvonne's head. She restrained herself. Instead she said, 'That's such a stupid thing to say.'

Yvonne's mouth turned down at the corners. She looked like a little girl who has just been told off by her parents. For a moment Neve actually suspected that she was going to cry but she soon regained her composure. Laurence, on the other hand, frowned and looked stern. Neve felt certain that he was going to tell her that she had been rude but at that precise moment the waiter arrived carrying their starters.

The conversation lapsed as the food was placed in front of them and for a while they were all too busy eating to say anything. Then Laurence began again. 'It won't be long before Yvonne and I have to start thinking about schools,' he said. 'Fortunately, the ones in our area are supposed to be very good.'

'Isn't Daniel a bit young for school?' Neve asked.

'Yes, but you need to have your options worked out in advance these days,' Laurence said.

It was a real surprise to hear her father talk like this. When Neve had been little he had been far too busy flying around the globe reporting on the world's trouble spots to give much thought to her education. Neve found herself remembering the time he had failed to turn up to see her in her school play. She must have been about eight years old and she had been really excited about being in a play. She had rehearsed very hard for weeks and on the night of the performance she had waited nervously on the stage, peeping out through the curtains as the audience filed into the school hall. Her father had been reporting from the other side of the world. It might have been Hong Kong, she wasn't sure. She had spoken to him two days earlier on the telephone and he had promised her solemnly that he would be there to see her perform, but when her mother came through the doors she was on her own. Neve could still remember how disappointed she had felt. A lump had come into her throat as she stood with the other children behind a screen, waiting to go on stage, and she had wanted to cry. All the fun had gone out of being in the play and her performance had suddenly become just something she had to get through. Afterwards, her mother had explained that her father had not been able to leave Hong Kong because the story he was working on was still developing. She had not understood what that meant at the time but it was an excuse she was often to hear repeated.

The morning after the school play her father had appeared on the television. It was the first time she could actually remember seeing him on the television, though he must have been on many times before. She could not even remember what the story was all about now, something to do with a politician who had told lies and had been found out. When she got to school her teacher had said, 'I saw your father on the television, Neve. You must be very proud of him.'

That was what it was like growing up with a famous father. Everyone expected her to be proud of him when what she wanted was for him to be proud of her. Everyone assumed, too, that she would turn out to be like him. That was why she had got so angry with Yvonne earlier on. Because she was not like him, not one bit. She was like herself.

Yvonne began talking about Daniel now and what a well behaved baby he was. Neve allowed the conversation to wash over her. She concentrated instead on the pizza which actually tasted extremely good. Her only worry was that she might not have room for the dessert. She had already noticed someone on the next table eating some tremendous-looking dish with ice-cream and cream and chocolate sauce. The thought of that made a lecture on child-care and infant education almost bearable.

But in the end even marble walls and good food weren't enough to make the evening work. Neve was disappointed. She had never expected it to be easy but she had been looking forward to seeing her father again. Even if he wasn't the best father in the world, he was her father and she hadn't seen him for two years. But it had simply not clicked between them. It was almost as if she were having dinner with two strangers.

The dessert, when it came, was delicious, but Neve was past enjoying it. She was beginning to feel tired. The evening had been a strain. All she wanted to do now was get back home. 'You must come soon to see our new house,' Laurence said after the waiter had taken his credit card. Neve nodded non-committally. 'It's your home too,' he added. He said this very deliberately, looking her straight in the eye. 'We want you to feel that. Don't we Yvonne?'

'Absolutely,' Yvonne agreed. 'You must come over all the time.'

During the drive home nobody spoke very much. Perhaps they were all tired. Neve sat in the back of the car looking out at the night lights of London but she was not really aware of what she was looking at. She was thinking about what it had been like when she was little and her mother and father had lived together perfectly happily, at least as far as she had known. It seemed like another world now. She could almost see herself, like a girl in a photograph from long ago. The girl was smiling. She had no idea that the cosy little world that surrounded her was soon going to break into little pieces and that as she grew older she would only be able to carry around fragments of memory from those days. Neve felt sorry for that girl. She did not know what was in store for her. How could she? She was just a child, lying in bed waiting for her father to tell her a story. And she knew which story it would be – her favourite, the one that had been made up just for her, the story about the little girl called Alissa who lived in a house with a balloon on the top, a house that could travel to any part of the world.

Suddenly she became aware that the car had come to a halt. 'Here we are sleepy-head,' Laurence said.

Neve realised that they had pulled up outside her house.

'I won't come in,' her father continued. 'We need to get back for the babysitter.'

'Right.' Neve was still half asleep.

'It's been lovely to see you again.'

'And you.' Neve opened the car door and got out. It seemed to have got much colder. She shivered.

Laurence rolled down the window. 'Kiss?' he said.

She kissed him on the cheek.

'You will remember what I said about our house? It's your home as well. Please don't forget that.'

'I won't. Thanks, and thanks for the meal. It was lovely.'

The front door opened. Her mother was standing there, waiting. She must have been watching out for the car, Neve realised. 'Bye, Dad,' she said.

'Bye, darling.' He closed the window and the car began to pull away. Neve had a glimpse of Yvonne looking back and waving. Then she turned and went inside out of the cold.

CHAPTER TWO

The Great Magician's daughter, whose name was Alissa, often asked her father to tell her the secret spells that controlled Balloon House. But he would only shake his head and say that she was not yet old enough. 'When will I be old enough?' she demanded, but the Great Magician did not answer. He was too busy with his spells and his books of magic.

'What kind of a name is Zed?' Neve asked. She was sitting in the studio watching her mother paint.

'I don't think it's his real name,' Judith replied.

The studio was really only a big shed in the back garden. Neve's mother had bought it after she and Laurence had separated. She's always wanted somewhere to paint. She had studied art before becoming a teacher but had given up painting when she had got pregnant with Neve. As she often observed, the studio was one of the positive things that had come out of her divorce.

Neve was not sure what she thought of her mother's paintings. They were pleasant to look at but she didn't really understand them. They seemed to be just splodges of colour. They obviously meant something to Judith, however, and occasionally she would talk about what she was doing. The painting she was working on today, for example, which was made up mostly of blues and purples, was, apparently inspired by a blue dress which she had worn when she was a little girl. She had told Neve this earlier that morning. 'I really loved that dress,' she had said. 'And the other day I was looking at some material in a shop and it reminded me of it. That started me off remembering all sorts of things.'

'And that's how the painting began?'

'Exactly.'

That was all very well. Neve could understand the connection between the blue dress and the blue painting. But what was the painting actually about? It wasn't a picture of a dress. It wasn't a picture of anything. According to her mother, her paintings weren't supposed to be pictures of anything. They were just themselves and that was all there was to it. Neve wasn't entirely convinced by this explanation. She had a suspicion that the paintings really did mean something but that her mother was not prepared to tell her what it was.

'I think his real name is Cedric,' her mother continued, making careful brushstrokes as she spoke.

'Cedric,' Neve said. 'That's terrible.'

'I expect that's why he calls himself Zed.'

Neve liked the studio. She liked the clutter. Inside the house everything was tidy but here chaos reigned. Painted and unpainted canvases were piled against one wall, together with wooden frames on which canvas was yet to be stretched. Tubes of paint spilled their contents out over the table which had been brought from the dining room to serve as her mother's workbench. Brushes, pencils, crayons, pastels and palette knives, were jumbled everywhere together with pots and jam-jars, coffee cups and saucers. The smell of paint and turpentine hung over everything. There was a freedom here that Neve found very attractive. What was more, her mother talked much more openly when she was painting. If Neve ever wanted to get round her mother and ask for something which she would not normally be allowed, the time to do it was when she was painting.

But that was not the reason why Neve was sitting in the studio on an upright wooden chair on that particular Saturday morning, swinging her legs and watching her mother paint. She was not there because she wanted something, or at least not something tangible. Perhaps she was just looking for reassurance. On Friday night her father had telephoned with a suggestion. He spoke first to Judith and then to Neve. He explained that Yvonne's son by her first marriage was staying with them. Normally he lived in Paris but he had come to visit London for a few days. He was a year or two older than Neve and his name was Zed. He wanted to see some of the sights of London and Laurence had suggested visiting the National Gallery. He thought that Neve might like to come along.

Neve had not been at all sure about the idea but her father was the sort of person who always managed to get his way in the end. So it was not surprising that Neve had found herself agreeing to meet them outside the National Gallery on Saturday afternoon. Now she was beginning to wish she had said no. Of course she wanted to see her father but she would much rather see him on his own. Laurence, however, had been very enthusiastic about the plan. It would be an opportunity for her to meet Daniel, he pointed out. He obviously regarded this as a bonus. That wasn't an opinion Neve shared. And then there was Zed, or Cedric, to give him his real name. What on earth did he think they would have in common? The more she thought about the prospect that lay ahead of her, the less she liked it.

'I think he's supposed to be very clever,' her mother went on.

'Great!' Neve said. 'A French boffin with a phoney name.'

Judith stopped painting and turned to look at Neve. She gave the impression of someone who was coming slowly out of a trance and having difficulty recognising her surroundings. 'I'm sure he's a very nice boy,' she said at last. 'You know you must try not to immediately assume the worst.'

'I'm not,' Neve protested.

'Yes you are,' Judith told her firmly. 'It's a habit you have. You look for the faults in people, instead of concentrating on their good points.'

Neve was stung by her mother's criticism. 'You make me sound really mean,' she said.

'Then I'm sorry,' Judith said, her normal, gentle manner reasserting itself. 'Just try to focus on the positive things about people.'

'I'll try,' Neve said, but without much conviction. It was easy for her mother to say that. She was a very positive person. Neve didn't find it quite so easy.

'I'm sure you're going to have a lovely afternoon,' her mother went on. 'I almost wish I was going with you. I haven't been to the National Gallery for years.' She turned back to her painting and began making tiny marks in one corner.

Neve said nothing. She watched her mother work with a kind of envy. Judith always seemed so sure about what she was doing. She was as clear about the right way to behave as she was about the shapes and colours of her paintings. To Neve, however, they were areas of equal uncertainty, and despite her mother's reassurance she was far from certain that it would turn out to be a lovely afternoon.

It occurred to Neve that if she were ever to write her autobiography, she could call it *Waiting For Dad* because she seemed to have spent so much of her life doing precisely that. She was standing outside the National Gallery looking in the direction of Charing Cross Station. It was not a warm day but at least the sun was shining and the fountains of

Trafalgar Square were sparkling in the sunlight. She had crossed the square fifteen minutes earlier, making her way through throngs of tourists and flocks of pigeons, past Nelson's Column and beside taxis, coaches and open-topped buses full of sight-seers. She had been exactly on time. The bells of St Martin's-in-the-Fields were ringing the hour as she went up the great stone staircase that leads to the gallery's main entrance. She had expected to find Laurence, Yvonne and Cedric – or Zed if that was what he really wanted to call himself – waiting outside. She should have known better. There was no sign of them.

She was standing between huge stone pillars beside a collection box with a sign inviting visitors to contribute towards the upkeep of the gallery. People streamed past speaking languages that she could only guess at. No doubt Yvonne would have been able to say what they were. A woman went by with a little girl. The girl was holding a balloon on the end of a length of string. She was so busy looking at the balloon that she kept bumping into passers-by. Neve found herself recalling her seventh birthday party. She remembered it very clearly because she had spent most of that party waiting for her father to turn up. He was away in Germany at the time, but, as usual, he had promised her faithfully that he would be back in time for the party. She had really wanted him to be there, more than anything in the world, but of course he had been delayed. He had phoned while she slept to say that he would be back by mid-morning but mid-morning had come and gone with no sign of her father. She had stood on the sofa in the front room looking out of the window, waiting for him to arrive. At three o'clock the guests had turned up and the party had begun. At six o'clock their parents had arrived to take them away again. They had each left clutching a balloon and a goody-bag that her mother had prepared beforehand. Finally, at half past seven her father had arrived armed with a present and an apology. She had not been interested in either. She would not even unwrap the present. In the end her mother had done it for her. She could not remember what it was now, a doll possibly. The main thing that she remembered, the real present that he had given her, was disappointment. And yet, at each milestone of her life after that, she had continued to hope that he would be there.

She had been waiting for nearly twenty-five minutes when she saw them coming. She noticed

Yvonne first. She was pushing a buggy with a baby in it. Beside her was a tall boy with dark hair. This, no doubt, was Zed. There was no sign of her father. Yvonne stopped at the foot of the steps and took Daniel out of the buggy. Zed picked the buggy up and they both walked up the stairs towards her.

They had not yet noticed Neve. She was standing behind one of the columns. As soon as Yvonne was in hearing range, she stepped out. 'Where's my dad?' she demanded.

Yvonne looked a bit flustered. 'I'm sorry we're so late,' she said.

'Where's my dad?' Neve repeated.

'I'm afraid he got held up,' Yvonne said. 'That's why we're late. We were waiting for him.'

Neve had known that would be the answer. She did not even know why she had bothered to ask. 'I've been standing here for the last half hour,' she said angrily.

'I know,' Yvonne said. 'I'm sorry. It wasn't anybody's fault.'

'Of course it was somebody's fault,' Neve said. 'It was his fault and it was yours for not getting here on time.'

'We didn't know for sure whether he would be

able to make it,' Yvonne explained.

'Then you shouldn't have waited,' Neve told her. 'You should have left him to make his own way here. At least then I wouldn't have had to stand around for half an hour in the cold.'

'I suppose we should have done that,' Yvonne agreed.

The weakness of her tone only made Neve even angrier. 'I didn't want to come in the first place,' she said. 'It was his idea. I'm not a tourist. I live here. I can visit the National Gallery any time I want to.' She knew, as she was saying this, that it was unfair on Zed. It wasn't his fault that he was a visitor to London, nor was it his fault that she had been kept waiting. But she didn't care about any of that. She was angry and she intended to have her say.

'You don't need to stay on my account,' Zed said. He spoke quietly but firmly. 'I can visit the gallery by myself. I don't need anybody else to come with me.' He had an unmistakable French accent but apart from that his English was perfect.

'Please let's not quarrel,' Yvonne said. She turned to Neve. 'I'm sorry,' she went on. 'You're quite right. It's my fault. I shouldn't have waited for Laurence.'

Neve did not want to accept her apology. She

wanted to continue to be angry. She wanted to turn and walk away, leaving them to their own devices. But she could no longer do that, not without putting herself in the wrong. She felt like someone playing chess who has just been checkmated. She could think of nothing to say. So she just gave a shrug.

'Shall we go inside then?' Yvonne asked.

They went into the entrance hall and waited while Yvonne handed in the buggy at the cloakroom and strapped Daniel into a sling. Zed made no attempt to talk to Neve but that was fine as far as she was concerned. When Yvonne was ready they went on under more pillars and up a flight of steps. At the top of the steps they were faced with a choice of rooms to enter. 'Does anybody have a preference?' Yvonne asked them. Neither of them said anything. Instead they followed her into the West Wing. A sign by the door informed them that it contained art from the sixteenth century.

The paintings inside were enormous and many of them seemed to be about religious subjects. There were pictures of Jesus wearing his crown of thorns and some of him on the cross. Neve did not find them particularly interesting. There were others which seemed to be based on mythical stories. They were full of nymphs and cupids. There seemed to be an enormous amount of naked flesh on display, most of it female. Neve felt slightly embarrassed to be staring at all these naked women in the company of a boy more or less her own age. She knew that she was being ridiculous thinking like that. This was art, but all the same, she hurried on past the pictures not waiting for the other two.

Yvonne stood in front of each picture in turn and surveyed it critically. She was keen not to miss anything. All the time she kept pointing things out to Daniel. 'Look at this man, Daniel,' Neve heard her say. 'Hasn't he got a funny face.'

She made her way into a room where paintings from a more modern era were kept. She found these much easier to enjoy. She stopped in front of one which she found immediately striking. It showed a young girl in a white silk dress that was so real you could almost reach out and touch it. She was wearing a blindfold and an old man in a long robe was talking to her. He had placed his hand on her arm. He was leading her, Neve realised with horror, towards a wooden block. She was going to put her head on that block. Beside the block an executioner was standing holding an axe. The painting was entitled *The Execution*

Of Lady Jane Grey.

Lady Jane Grey looked about sixteen or seventeen years old. She had the sweetest face that Neve could imagine, the face of someone who wouldn't hurt a fly. Nevertheless she was going to be killed in the most dreadful manner. Neve stared at the painting in horror but she was unable to take her eyes off it. She almost felt as if she were the girl in the picture, as if she were waiting to be executed for a crime she had not committed.

'Do you like it?' a voice said.

She turned to see that Zed was standing beside her.

'It's horrible,' she replied.

'Yes,' he agreed. 'But fascinating, too, don't you think?'

She didn't want to agree with him but she nodded all the same.

'It's by a French painter,' Zed went on. He sounded as if he were proud of this.

'I don't think it can be,' Neve told him. 'It's from English history. I think she was a queen who only ruled for a few days.'

Zed pointed to the notice beside the picture. 'Paul Delaroche,' he said.

Neve felt annoyed and stupid at the same time. If only she had looked more carefully she would have seen the name of the painter and she would not have made a fool of herself. She immediately walked away leaving Zed to admire the picture on his own.

It had been arranged that they would go back to Laurence's and Yvonne's house for dinner. As usual, despite her misgivings, Neve found herself falling in with this plan. To say no she did not want to have dinner with them would have required too much effort. So they took a cab back to the comfortable suburb of North London where Laurence and Yvonne had chosen to set up house. Neve sat staring out of the window throughout the journey, still thinking about the painting she had seen, wondering what it would be like to stumble blindfolded and innocent towards your own execution.

Laurence was in the kitchen when they got back. He was wearing a striped chef's apron and was clearly in the middle of preparing a meal. A saucepan of something that smelled good was simmering on the hob. Little mounds of diced vegetables were piled up on the chopping board in front of him. He greeted them enthusiastically, almost theatrically, like a television chef addressing the audience. 'How are the culture vultures?' he asked, smiling broadly. 'Did you have a good time?' He seemed to have entirely forgotten that he had been meant to accompany them to the gallery, that the whole thing had been his idea in the first place.

But Neve had no intention of allowing him to get away with that. 'Where were you?' she demanded.

Laurence spread his hands wide in a gesture of innocence. 'Sorry about that,' he said. 'Work, I'm afraid. You know what it's like.'

'I know what's it's like standing around in the cold waiting for people who don't turn up, if that's what you mean,' Neve said.

Laurence raised his eyebrows. 'Sorry,' he said. 'There wasn't anything I could do about it.'

'Yes there was,' Neve insisted. 'You could have turned up on time like you promised.' She stood in the middle of the kitchen staring defiantly at him. For once she was going to confront him, make him explain himself. She had made up her mind about that on the journey home. He was not going to get away with it quite so easily this time.

'I couldn't, Neve,' Laurence said. He spoke calmly and softly. 'What I had to do was urgent. I didn't have any alternative.'

'What was so urgent about it?'

'I can't explain that.'

'Because there wasn't anything, that's why.'

'Neve, your dad is working on something very important,' Yvonne said.

Neve turned to look at her. She was holding the baby over her shoulder, rocking him gently as she spoke. Neve felt a huge force of anger building up inside her. She wanted to say, 'This has got nothing to do with you. It's between me and him.' She struggled to control herself. She could feel tears of anger and frustration welling up inside her. She turned back to her dad. 'Your work always has to come first, doesn't it?' she said.

Laurence looked at her for a long time without saying anything. Then he said, 'Neve, I think you should try to calm down.'

'I'm perfectly calm.'

'You don't sound calm,' Yvonne said.

Neve could no longer control herself. She turned on Yvonne. 'Can you just stay out of it!' she shouted.

Yvonne looked as if she had been hit in the face. She opened her mouth to speak and then shut it again. For a brief moment Neve felt a flush of pleasure at the reaction she had caused. Then the pleasure died away as she saw the anger on her father's face.

'Neve, there's no need to behave like that,' he said. 'I think you should apologise to Yvonne.'

'It doesn't matter,' Yvonne said quickly.

It was so hard not to cry. Neve's lips were trembling. But she wasn't going to let it happen. She struggled to speak. 'Why do I have to apologise?' she demanded. 'You're the one who didn't turn up.'

'And I've said I'm sorry,' Laurence said, speaking in that same measured tone that was somehow even more infuriating than if he had been shouting at her. 'What more do you want me to do?'

'I want you to tell me what was so important that you couldn't keep your promise,' Neve said.

Laurence thought about this. 'All right,' he said at last. 'Let's sit down and talk about it in a civilised fashion.' He pulled out a chair and sat down at the kitchen table. Neve did the same.

'I'm just going to put Daniel to sleep,' Yvonne said, disappearing out of the room. Zed followed her, leaving Neve and her father alone together.

'OK,' Laurence said when the others had gone.

'I'm sorry I didn't turn up. I've said it before but I'll say it again, but I had very important reasons.'

'More important than me, I suppose,' Neve said.

'That's so unfair,' her father said. 'Nothing in the world is more important to me than you.'

'Except your job,' Neve pointed out.

Laurence looked hurt. 'Listen, Neve, if I could explain further I would, but I just can't.'

'Because there isn't anything to explain.'

'Because I'd be putting you in danger.'

'What's that supposed to mean?'

He shook his head. 'Nothing. I shouldn't have said it.'

Neve stared at him defiantly. 'That's it, is it? End of discussion?'

'I can't say any more,' he told her.

'You mean you don't want to.'

Her father opened his mouth as if to speak, then closed it again. At last he seemed to come to a decision. 'If I tell you why I couldn't come I want you to promise not to repeat it to anyone else. Agreed?'

'I suppose so.'

'"I suppose so" isn't good enough. Do you promise not to tell anyone else?'

Neve felt certain that he was making a big deal

about nothing but she nodded her head anyway. 'OK.'

'All right then.' Laurence said. He paused as if he was choosing his words carefully. 'I'm involved in an investigation into aid fraud. Do you know what that is?'

Neve shook her head.

'Money that developed countries like ours give to developing countries to help them fight poverty and disease and develop their economies, that's called aid. OK?'

She nodded.

'I'm not talking about small amounts of money here, like you might put in a collection box. I'm talking about millions donated by one government to another. Do you understand?'

'I'm not stupid,' Neve told him. 'Of course I understand.'

Laurence sighed again. It seemed to Neve he was acting like a teacher explaining something to a not very bright pupil. 'I'm not saying you're stupid,' he told her. 'I'm just explaining what I'm doing, like you asked me to. All right?'

Neve nodded. He managed to sound both annoyed and wounded at the same time, she thought. That was so typical of him. He was the one who was in the wrong. He was the one who hadn't turned up for the umpteenth time in her life. And yet here he was acting like he had been hard done by.

'Well, aid is a very important thing,' he continued. 'It can mean the difference between life and death to huge numbers of people, not just when there's been some sort of natural disaster but at any time. Large numbers of people depend on aid. I'm not saying that's how it should be. It's just a fact. Right?'

Neve wondered when he was going to get to the point.

'The thing is,' he went on, 'sometimes aid doesn't get to where it's supposed to. It gets siphoned off somewhere along the line. Those people get cheated.'

'So where does it go?'

'Into the bank accounts of wealthy individuals. That's what I'm investigating. And that's what couldn't wait.'

Neve was still not convinced. 'But if you've been investigating this for over a year now, what difference would one afternoon make?' she demanded.

Laurence smiled. She got the feeling he had been waiting for her to ask that question. 'All the difference in the world,' he said. 'I'm getting very close, Neve. Very close indeed.'

'Close to what?'

'Close to the source, to where it all starts. It's been like untangling a huge knot. You keep thinking you've done it and then you find there's another bit left to unravel. But it's dangerous. That's why I didn't want to talk about it with you. Or with anyone for that matter. The fewer people who know what I'm doing the better. I haven't even really discussed it with Yvonne.' She was surprised to hear him say that and she felt for the first time that what he was telling her might be true.

'In what way is it dangerous?' she asked.

He shrugged. 'The people that I'm investigating have a lot to lose.'

'Do they know about you?' Neve asked.

Laurence shook his head. 'No.'

'Are you sure?'

'Pretty sure.'

'What would they do if they found out?'

'They're not going to find out,' Laurence said. 'Because it's something I keep very quiet about. That's why it's important that you don't discuss this with anyone else, even your mother.'

Neve looked uncertain.

'I don't want her worrying, that's all. Promise you won't mention it.'

'I promise,' Neve said, a little reluctantly.

Yvonne came back into the room just then. Laurence looked up. 'Is he asleep?' he asked.

'Yes.'

'Great. Well I think it's time I got back to my cooking,' he said. He stood up and went back to the chopping board. That was it, as far as he was concerned. He had given his explanation, the baby was asleep, now he could go back to chopping vegetables.

'Perhaps you'd like to wait in the sitting room, while I finish off,' he said.

Neve was dismissed. She got up and went out of the kitchen. She walked past the dining room and caught a glimpse, through the half-open door of a table laid with a white cloth, plates and knives and forks. Things were much more formal here than they were at home. She presumed that was the influence of Yvonne.

She went through into the sitting room. There were two sofas at either end of the room facing each other. On one of these Zed was sitting reading a book. She had forgotten about him. So this was where he had gone. He looked up when she came into the room, then carried on reading. Neve walked over to the other sofa and sat down. She did not look directly at Zed but she noticed the cover of the book he was reading. The writing was in French. She felt a slight envy of his ability to use two different languages with such ease. He shut the book and put it down. 'Did you enjoy the visit to the National Gallery?' he asked.

Neve was surprised by his question. She had not expected him to try to make conversation. She shook her head. 'No I didn't,' she said.

'Not even the picture of Lady Jane Grey?'

'It was all right.'

Although his English was perfect there was a quality about it that was ever so slightly stilted, a little bit too formal. Maybe he takes after his mother, Neve decided, recalling the perfectly positioned knives and forks in the dining room.

'Is it true that your mother's a painter?' he asked.

Neve felt slightly irritated to hear him say this. 'Who told you that?' she asked.

'Your father.'

'Well she's not,' Neve said. 'She's a teacher.'

'Sorry,' Zed said. 'I must have misunderstood.'

Neve relented a little. 'She paints at weekends,' she said. 'But it's just for herself.' That was what her mother always said whenever anyone asked her about her painting. 'It's something I do for myself. It's mine and no one can take it away from me.'

Zed nodded as if he knew perfectly well what she meant.

Perhaps she should try to be nicer to him, Neve decided. After all, he was doing his best. But at that moment Yvonne came into the room. She was holding Daniel. 'I'm afraid he didn't stay asleep for very long,' she said. 'I think he knew there were other people here. He wanted a bit of the action.' She sat down beside Neve. 'He's been ever so good today,' she said. 'Some babies might have made a terrible fuss about being hungry in a great big art gallery. But not Daniel. He's been a very good boy, haven't you?' She put her face close to Daniel's when she said this and he chortled with pleasure. 'Would you like to hold him?' she asked Neve.

Neve did not want to hold him. 'I might drop him,' she pointed out.

'No you won't,' Yvonne assured her. 'It's easy. Here.' She lifted Daniel off her lap and put him in Neve's. 'You just support his head. That's it.' Neve found that she was holding Daniel whether she liked it or not. His eyes, which seemed incredibly big, were looking up at her gravely. 'This is Neve. She's your sister,' Yvonne told him.

'I'm not his sister,' Neve protested. 'I'm his half-sister.'

Daniel's expression was beginning to change. It was as if he sensed that Neve was not entirely happy about the arrangement. Neve suspected that if she held him for very long he might start crying.

Just then Laurence came into the room. 'Food's ready,' he announced. He saw Neve holding Daniel. 'I see you two are getting to know each other,' he said. He crossed the room and looked down at Daniel who was beginning to look distinctly cross.

'He's not looking very happy,' Neve said. 'I think he needs to go back to his mother.'

'He's just thinking,' Laurence said. 'He's like you. He frowns when he thinks.'

Neve did not want to hear him say that. He was trying to make out that they were all one big happy family when they were not. She had not wanted to hold Daniel in the first place. Now, to be told that he was like her was more than she was prepared to put up with. She put him firmly back on his mother's lap and stood up. 'Let's go and eat, then,' she said.

They went into the dining room and sat down. Yvonne placed Daniel in a cradle on the floor, where he could watch them eating. He seemed content with this. Laurence had cooked breast of chicken in some sort of fancy sauce with rice.

'What do you think?' Laurence asked her as soon as she had tasted the chicken.

'It's nice,' she said. She knew he wanted her to say that it was magnificent. She didn't bother. He had already got someone for that role.

Right on cue Yvonne said, 'This is wonderful, Laurence.' She turned to Neve. 'Your father is such a good cook.'

'He's all right,' Neve said.

'He's more than all right,' Yvonne insisted.

Neve wanted to say, 'Yes but he has to make a song and dance about it.' Her mother cooked every day. The food was always good but she didn't expect anyone to stand up and applaud. Neve's feelings of anger towards her father had begun to resurface. It was that remark about Daniel looking like her that had started it all off again. He was so pleased with himself and his new wife and baby. It didn't occur to him that Neve might look at things differently.

'Neve,' Laurence said, 'You're not still sulking are you?'

'I haven't been sulking,' Neve told him.

'Not even just a tiny bit?' he asked, smiling.

'Not even a tiny bit,' she said. She was not going to let him turn it into a joke.

'What spices did you put in this sauce?' Yvonne said. She looked at Laurence as if she could hardly believe his brilliance.

'Lemon grass,' Laurence said. 'It makes all the difference.'

'It's very nice,' Zed said. It was the first time he had spoken since they had sat down at the table.

'Thank you,' Laurence said. Then he looked around at them all. 'So. How was the National Gallery?'

'It was wonderful,' Yvonne told him.

'You think everything's wonderful,' Neve said. She had said it before she could stop herself. She didn't mean it to sound quite so bad. It was the truth, that was all. Yvonne did think everything was wonderful. The National Gallery was wonderful, the food was wonderful, Daniel was wonderful, and, of course, her father was wonderful. He was the most wonderful of all.

Everyone stopped eating. Laurence's fork stopped halfway to his mouth. 'Neve,' he said, 'there's no need to be like that.'

'Like what?' she asked.

'Unpleasant.'

'I wasn't being unpleasant.'

Laurence sighed. His expression was that of a man who was suffering patiently. He put on his softest voice. 'Come on, Alissa,' he said.

The moment he said that the emotional temperature of the room changed abruptly. Neve felt a wave of indignation rushing through her. Alissa was his pet name for her, a name he had called her when she was little. It was the name of a girl in a story which she had loved listening to. How dare he pull something of her childhood out like this and use it to try and charm her.

'What did you call her?' Yvonne asked.

Laurence turned to her. 'Alissa,' he said. 'It's the name of a girl in a story...'

He was going to tell her about it, describe how little Neve had loved listening to the story. She couldn't stop him. He was going to broadcast her secrets over the dinner table. Well she wasn't going to sit there and listen to it. She stood up. As she did so, her elbow caught Yvonne's glass of wine and knocked it over.

Neve stared for a moment as the red wine ran over the table cloth, staining it like blood. Then she ran out of the room. She could feel the tears coming. She went straight up the stairs and into the bathroom. She locked the door behind her. Then her control disappeared. She sat on the edge of the bath and sobbed.

When she was finished she looked at herself in the mirror. Her face was blotchy. It was obvious that she had been crying. She splashed water into her eyes several times, then looked in the mirror again. She didn't look much better. She dried her face, then thought about going downstairs and facing them all again. It was a daunting prospect.

She couldn't stay in the bathroom all evening, however. She opened the door and looked out. There was nobody waiting there. She stepped outside. She still did not want to go downstairs. The closer she came to doing it, the harder it got. Just along the corridor from the bathroom was another door which was open. The light was on. It was Laurence's study. She stood in the doorway for a moment. Then she stepped inside.

*

She was a strange, difficult, sulky and irritating girl. That was what Zed was thinking. She seemed to have been trying all day to wreck things, to make everybody as miserable as she was. And yet, he had a feeling that he could like her, that he could be friends with her. There was something about her that made him want to know her properly.

It was strange to have these two contradictory thoughts going on at the same time, but Zed often found that. An idea occurred to him and he was just becoming convinced that it was true, when he clearly saw the opposite possibility. His mother sometimes told him that he thought too much, as if thinking could be a bad thing. And maybe she was right. He certainly found that it got in the way sometimes. He wanted to say something and then he thought: no that sounds stupid. Which was why he found himself feeling more sorry for Neve than angry with her. She was finding her life hard going. He knew that feeling.

His mother had mopped up the spilt wine with kitchen towel. Luckily it had gone on the table cloth and not on her clothes.

'Will it stain?' Laurence asked.

'It doesn't matter,' Yvonne said. 'It's only a table cloth.'

'Yes, but she shouldn't have behaved like that. She's been absolutely dreadful since you all came back.'

'The whole day has been like that,' Yvonne told him.

'I should go and speak to her,' Laurence said, but he sounded as if he did not really want to.

'I'll talk to her,' Zed suggested. He had no idea why he had suddenly said that, except that he strongly suspected Laurence would only make things worse.

'Would you?' Laurence looked distinctly hopeful.

'Of course.' Zed stood up.

'Thanks very much.'

Now that his suggestion had been accepted, Zed immediately found himself regretting it. He went out of the room and stood in the hallway, uncertain what to do next. Then he went up the stairs slowly trying to think of what he would say when he found Neve.

The bathroom door was open. He peered inside. She was not there. He stood there for a moment wondering where she could have gone when he heard a sniff coming from the room next door. He walked along the hall and knocked on the door.

'Go away!' Neve's voice said.

'It's me,' Zed told her.

'Please go away.'

Zed felt ridiculous but he could not just go back downstairs and say that she wouldn't talk to him. 'I only wanted to know if you are all right,' he said.

'Of course I'm not all right!'

'I'm sorry.'

'What are you sorry for?'

'For making you behave like a tourist today.'

There was a long silence. 'Can I come in?' he asked.

'If you really want to.'

He opened the door. Neve was standing beside the wall. It was obvious from her face that she had been crying. 'This has got nothing to do with you,' she told him, when he stepped inside.

'The visit to the gallery was because of me.'

'That's not the reason I was upset.'

'Then what is?'

She sighed. 'You wouldn't understand.'

'Try me.'

She gave him a long look, as if she was trying to

decide whether it was worth talking to him. Then she seemed to make up her mind. She turned and pointed to a picture that was hanging in a frame on the wall above her father's desk. 'Look at this,' she said.

He crossed the room and stood beside her, looking at the picture. It appeared to be a child's drawing of a house, done in felt-tip pen.

'I did that.'

He had not expected this. He had no idea why she was showing him the picture. 'It's a house.' He couldn't think of anything else to say.

'It's a house in a story my dad made up,' she told him. 'The story was called "Balloon House". That's meant to be a balloon on top of the house.'

Zed looked more carefully. Above the house someone had drawn a circle and made childish attempts to colour it in. He had thought, at first, that it was meant to be the sun. But there were lines coming down from it to the house. They were obviously meant to be the ropes that attached the balloon to the house.

'How old were you when you drew it?' he asked. He did not know why he asked this. It did not matter how old she had been, but it kept the conversation going.

'Four or five,' she said. 'I don't remember, exactly.'

'Your father must have been very pleased with it.'

'Why do you say that?'

He was surprised by her question. The answer seemed so obvious. But she was looking at him keenly, as if it was very important to hear him say it. 'Because he has framed it and put it on his wall.'

She was still looking hard at him, as if she was not sure whether he really meant what he said. Then she shrugged. 'Maybe,' she said. 'Anyway, it's a story about a great magician who has this magical house that can sail anywhere in the world and he goes off on all these adventures with his daughter.'

'I see.' He did not see at all. What on earth had this got to do with anything?

'Her name was Alissa.' She looked at him meaningfully.

'Sorry?' He did not know what he was supposed to say.

'That's the name my father just called me, when I was downstairs.'

'Oh.' Now he was beginning to understand.

'It was something special, something from my childhood. He shouldn't have called me that in front of everyone.'

'I see.'

She looked irritated. 'I knew you wouldn't understand,' she said.

'But I do understand.'

'Maybe.'

'No really,' he insisted. 'I do understand. Listen, you have told me something about yourself. I will tell you something about myself. OK?'

She nodded. 'All right.'

'I had this dream once. It was not long after my mother and father told me that they were splitting up. They said they had something important to say so we all sat down and then they announced that they were separating. It was a shock for me. I didn't expect it at all.'

Neve didn't say anything but she was listening.

'A few nights later I dreamed that I was climbing. I used to go climbing with my father sometimes. Anyway I was on a ledge on a cliff-face. I leaned away from the ledge, putting all my weight on the rope that was holding me. Suddenly the rope snapped and I started falling. That was when I woke up.'

'That's horrible,' Neve said.

'Yes it was, but I knew that the dream was really about my mother and father splitting up. I realise that it's not obviously about that, but underneath it is. That was what I decided the next day.'

'It's your dream,' she said. 'You should know.'

'I wrote a poem about it,' he went on. He felt embarrassed telling her this but it was essential if she was to understand the point of the story. She made no comment so he carried on. 'I left it on the table in my room. That day my mother tidied my room when I was out. She found the poem and read it.'

'How do you know she read it?'

'She told me. She said, "By the way, I liked your poem."'

'Were you angry?'

'Of course, but do you know what I was most angry about?'

'What?'

'She didn't guess what the poem was really about.'

Neve looked unconvinced. 'You said, yourself, it's not obvious.'

'Not to an outsider,' he said. 'But she's my mother. Three days earlier she and my father had announced that they were separating. I have a dream in which I have fallen down a cliff and she doesn't put the two together.'

Neve nodded. 'I see what you mean,' she said.

'But maybe she did see the connection and just didn't mention it. Have you thought about that?'

'If she knew what the dream was really about and didn't say anything then that's even worse. But she didn't. She's my mother. I know what she's like.'

They were both silent then. Zed wasn't sure whether she understood what he had been trying to say. When he told the story it did not sound very important. Many people would think, as Neve had done, that it was not so bad that his mother did not understand what the dream had meant. And maybe it wasn't. But things were always like that between them. She noticed what went on in her own life but she did not pay any real attention to what went on in his.

'Is that why you live with your father?' Neve suddenly asked.

He shook his head. 'My father is even worse,' he said. 'He is interested in only two things: his job and climbing.'

'My dad's only interested in his job,' Neve said. Then she paused as if something had only just occurred to her. 'Why did you come up here after me?' she asked him.

Zed shrugged. He did not fully know the answer to

this himself. It was on the tip of his tongue to say that he had felt sorry for her but he guessed that an answer like that would not go down well with Neve. 'I thought it might help,' he said, after a moment.

Neve considered this. Then she said, 'It did.'

'Good. Do you feel like going downstairs again, now?' Zed asked. Sooner or later, he suspected, Laurence or his mother might come up to see what was happening. He could imagine them saying something stupid and the whole thing starting again.

'OK. Thanks, by the way.' She smiled. It was the first time he had seen her smile all day long. She looked like a completely different person.

CHAPTER THREE

At last, one day Alissa's chance came. The Great Magician had been so busy that he had forgotten all about his daughter's birthday. Now he tried to make it up to her. 'Choose whatever you wish as a birthday present,' he told her. Immediately Alissa replied, 'Tell me the Unfathomable Word.' Her father was angry when she said this, for the Unfathomable World was the strongest of all his spells, but a magician cannot go back on his promise. He leaned over and whispered in her ear, 'Meeonissibar'. As he did so, Balloon House shook from the roof top down to its very foundations. 'Speak it beyond these walls and you shall have help wherever you are,' he told her, 'but only do so if all else fails, for the Unfathomable Word also brings death and destruction.'

'Do you think Dad's job is dangerous?' Neve asked.
   They were in the studio again in the middle of the

familiar clutter of painting. Neve was sitting on her usual chair watching her mother wielding her paint-brush, carefully and precisely, to produce the strange swirling shapes which Neve found so mysterious.

'There's always an element of risk in a job like his I suppose,' Judith said. 'Why?'

'No particular reason,' Neve replied. She had told her mother about her father's failure to turn up at the National Gallery but she had said nothing about the conversation that had taken place in the kitchen afterwards. After all, she had promised that she would not discuss it.

Judith stopped painting and looked at Neve. 'So what made you ask?'

Neve shrugged. 'I don't know,' she said quickly. 'I just wondered.'

Judith raised one eyebrow.

'I just thought, you know, he's always digging around trying to find out things that other people want to keep hidden. He must make a lot of enemies.'

Judith thought about this. 'That's not the sort of thing that worries your dad,' she said. 'He just carries on with what he's doing, regardless of what other people think. Anyway, I shouldn't worry about him.

He's old enough to take care of himself.' She went back to painting, and for a time there was silence between them.

'So what did you think of Zed then?' Judith asked, after a little while.

'I don't know really,' Neve said. 'I think he's all right. I just wish...'

'You just wish what?'

Neve sighed. She hadn't really meant to go into all this but she had started now so she had to continue. 'I just wish I'd been a bit nicer to him,' she said. She was not happy with the way the day had gone. She had been in a bad mood – that wasn't entirely her fault, her father was mostly to blame – but she knew she had been a misery, and Zed had been really nice to her in the evening when she had made a fool of herself by rushing out of the room like that. 'I feel a bit guilty, I suppose' she added.

Judith gave a wry smile. 'A little bit of guilt won't kill you,' she said, 'so long as you use it positively.'

'How can I do that?' Neve replied. 'There's nothing positive about feeling guilty.'

'Why don't you offer to show him around London?'

Neve looked at her in surprise. 'Do you really

think I should?' she asked.

'I'm not saying you should,' Judith pointed out, 'I'm just making a suggestion.'

'On my own?'

'Is that so outrageous?' Judith said. 'Honestly, Neve, you make me feel like an irresponsible mother. I simply thought that it would be a nice thing to do. After all, he's a young person in a foreign country. He's got no one of his own generation to talk to. I expect he'd like to see another side of London from what his mother thinks is exciting. You could always ask someone else to come along as well. What about Holly?'

That was a possibility. Holly was a family friend. Her mother and Judith had grown up together. She lived on the other side of London now but they had lived very close by when Neve was little and she and Holly had played together as toddlers. The friendship had survived even after Holly's mother had uprooted the family and gone to live on the other side of the Thames. They met regularly in the centre of London. Sometimes they sat in a café, sometimes they went clothes shopping together. 'It might be a bit weird for Holly, though,' Neve said.

'Well she can always say no,' Judith pointed out.

'I suppose so.'

Judith stood back and looked at the canvas she was painting. 'What do you think?' she asked.

'It's nice.'

'I don't want it to be nice,' Judith said. 'I want it to be good.'

'Well it's good then.'

Judith shook her head. 'It needs more blue,' she said. 'Did you enjoy the meal, apart from your argument, that is?'

'The meal was pretty good. It wasn't really an argument. I just left the room because Dad really annoyed me.'

'I know what he can be like,' Judith said, 'but believe me, it's not worth getting annoyed about.'

Neve shook her head. 'Sometimes it is,' she said. Then she got up and went out of the studio.

Holly really liked the idea of showing Zed around. She was immediately enthusiastic. 'It will be fun,' she said. 'We'll be looking at London through the eyes of a stranger.'

'I hadn't thought about it like that, exactly,' Neve said.

'I read an article in a magazine,' Holly went on,

'called "Twenty Ways To Enjoy Yourself For Free". Most of it was rubbish but one of the things it suggested was to go around the place you live with someone from a different country. You get a chance to look at everything with fresh eyes.'

'I suppose that's true,' Neve said. 'Anyway, I thought we could go round Covent Garden, but I haven't phoned him yet. He might not like the idea.'

'Are you crazy?' Holly said. 'He's a boy in a foreign city. He doesn't know anyone. Two attractive girls phone him up and ask him if he wants to look around the city, and you think he might not like the idea.'

'He's my step-brother,' Neve pointed out. Sometimes Holly needed to be reined in.

'I know he is,' Holly said. 'All I'm saying is, of course he'll accept.'

But asking Zed was not as easy as Holly imagined. It took Neve quite a long time to psyche herself up enough to make the phone call. She went upstairs where she would not be disturbed and picked up the telephone.

It was Yvonne who answered. She sounded exactly as she had the first time Neve had spoken to her. At least she was not the kind to hold grudges. If she was surprised when Neve asked to speak to Zed, she certainly didn't show it. She went to fetch him without any comment.

'Hello,' Zed said a moment later.

'Hi. It's me, Neve. I just wondered whether you wanted to see Covent Garden.' It wasn't how she had expected to begin. She had rather blurted out what she wanted to say.

Zed hesitated. 'With you, you mean?' he asked.

'Yes, and my friend, Holly. She's a family friend,' Neve explained. 'We often meet in Covent Garden. It's a nice place to sit and see London. But if you don't fancy it,' she hurried on, sensing that perhaps this was not going well.'

'I do fancy it,' Zed interrupted, 'but I don't want to make you behave like a tourist.'

Neve almost winced when he said that. It was fair enough of course, after what she had said.

'Don't worry,' she told him. 'It's not being a tourist, it's just, you know...' she searched for a phrase, 'hanging out.'

'OK then. That would be good,' Zed said. 'Thank you very much.' He still sounded grave and formal. Perhaps it was the result of speaking in a second language, or perhaps it was simply his personality, she was not sure. But he also sounded pleased.

*

The following Saturday they all met at Charing Cross station. Holly and Zed were both waiting when Neve got off the train. They were standing separately among the passengers facing the Departures Board. Holly was the first to see Neve. She smiled, waved eagerly and began walking towards her. Then Zed also saw her. He came over to join them. Neve realised that it was up to her to make the introductions.

Holly had dark hair, olive skin and eyes that flashed with pleasure whenever she got enthusiastic about something, which was frequently. She was looking at Zed with those eyes right now. She had got a new haircut. It was all spiky and untidy-on-purpose and Neve felt almost dowdy beside her. She stood there hesitantly, starting to wish she had not suggested this meeting in the first place. Then she pulled herself together. This is just what happens when you introduce two friends to each other, she told herself. She realised that they were both waiting for her to say something so she began. 'This is Holly, this is Zed.'

'Bonjour,' Holly said.

Neve looked at her in surprise. She had not

expected Holly to begin speaking in French.'

Zed smiled. 'Bonjour,' he replied. Then he immediately said something else in French, speaking so
quickly that it was difficult to catch a word.

Holly laughed. 'That's all I can say,' she admitted.

Zed smiled back at her. 'It's a start,' he said. Then
he turned to Neve. 'So where are we headed?'

'The Bagel House,' she told him.

'Where else?' Holly chorused.

Neve and Holly had discovered the Bagel House
on one of their walks together around Covent
Garden. You had to go through a series of back-
streets and then along a little alleyway and suddenly
you found yourself in a courtyard. On all sides there
were shops selling clothes and jewellery, candlesticks
and incense, books, bags and beads. In the middle of
them all nestled the Bagel House. You could chose
your bagel and then sit at one of the tables outside,
watching the world go by.

Zed was suitably impressed when they arrived. 'I
would never have found this place on my own,' he
admitted, as they stood at the counter making up
their minds what to order. Neve had a tuna and
sweetcorn bagel. Holly opted for turkey with roasted
aubergines and tomato salsa. 'Wow!' Neve said.

'That's a weird combination.' Holly usually had nothing but honey.

'I'm feeling adventurous today,' Holly told her.

For some reason, Neve found Holly's adventurousness slightly threatening. Like her haircut, it was a bold choice and Neve couldn't help feeling that it made *her* look a bit conventional by comparison.

'Out with it!' Holly said, pointing her finger in a jokey gesture at Zed. 'What are you going to have?'

But Zed would not be hurried. He studied the menu carefully. At last he made up his mind and ordered a cream cheese bagel. Neve was glad that his choice was as straightforward as her own.

'You mean you're not going to try the tomato salsa?' Holly asked.

'You can tell us about it,' Zed said.

It was a diplomatic answer, Neve thought, and typical of Zed. Even when he relaxed he was still careful about what he said. It was as if he had been brought up more strictly than she had.

They sat down at one of the little tables that looked out on to the courtyard. This was the first warm day, the first day that it was actually possible to sit outside at a café table. The tops of the buildings opposite towered four storeys above the courtyard.

They were draped with plants which hung from balconies beneath tall french windows. The air of the courtyard was filled with a mixture of scents: incense, bagels, coffee, cigarette smoke and traffic fumes. It was a strange, and somehow exciting combination. As they sat there the sun came out from behind a cloud and lit up the courtyard. It was almost magical.

'We thought you might like to see some of our favourite shops,' Holly said.

It seemed to Neve that Holly was in danger of taking charge. She decided to resist. 'Or we could just explore instead,' she suggested.

Zed looked from one of them to the other. 'What sort of shops do you like?' he asked.

'Clothes shops, mostly,' Holly told him.

'Let's just explore,' he said.

After they had eaten their bagels they sat for a while drinking coffee and making up stories about the people who passed through the courtyard. Most of them probably worked in the shops and studios nearby. Others were quite obviously tourists, like the middle-aged couple dressed in their best casuals who walked slowly through the square, peering at a map and pointing things out to each other. 'You could look like them if you're not careful,' Holly told Zed.

She meant it as a joke but it fell flat. Zed looked slightly uncomfortable and Neve felt embarrassed, remembering what she had said about behaving like a tourist. 'Time to start exploring,' she said, standing up.

Holly wanted to go to Frenzy, which was one of their favourite shops but Zed was not very interested. He put his head inside the door and looked around but he did not want to go in.

To Neve's surprise, the shop that really fascinated him was the fossil shop. She had known it was there, walked past it many times, but had never bothered to go inside. It was full of lumps of rock, and bits of creatures that had lived millions of years ago. That was all there was to it. But Zed looked really pleased when he noticed it.

'Why do you want to go in there?' Holly asked him.

'I like rocks,' Zed said. 'They're practically the oldest thing on the planet.'

Holly looked at Neve, shrugged in a better-humour-him gesture and they all went inside.

In the shop there were trays full of rocks with pieces of crystal inside them, rocks that contained tiny specks of metal and glittered when you held them up and rocks that had long ago become prisons for prehistoric shellfish and plants. 'My father used to tell me all about rocks when we went climbing,' Zed said. He was talking just to Neve now. 'He knows all about them. He's a hydro-geologist.'

'I don't know what a hydro-geologist is,' Neve confessed.

Zed smiled. 'Not many people do, except other hydro-geologists - and their families,' he said.

'Look at this!' Holly exclaimed, holding up a petrified starfish. 'Fancy having one of these on your dressing-table!'

After they had looked at the shops, they went on a tour of the street entertainers. There was a string quartet playing Beethoven, a man on a unicycle juggling coloured skittles and a mime artist.

Holly had been right. It was fun. All of these sights were there every day but like most Londoners, Neve took no notice of them. Today, however, she had a reason to notice and she was enjoying herself. She was surprised at how quickly six o'clock came around. When she had made the arrangements Neve had wondered whether she had allowed too much time, but now she was sorry that it was over.

'Thank you very much,' Zed said to them both with his usual courtesy.

Holly giggled. He looked at her, slightly surprised. 'You're so polite,' she told him. Then an idea seemed to strike her. 'When are you going back?' she asked.

'Friday,' Zed told her.

She put her hand in her bag and brought out her address book and a pen. 'Give me your address in France,' she told him. 'I might look you up when I go over.'

The next day, when Holly phoned for a chat, Neve said, 'I didn't know you were planning a trip to Paris.' She had been too surprised at the time to say anything as Zed had written his address in neat, sloping handwriting in Holly's book.

'Why not?' Holly replied. 'It's only a train journey.'

'But are you definitely going?' For some reason Neve wanted to know for sure.

'Maybe,' Holly said. She had phoned up, it soon became obvious, in the hope that Neve might be thinking of arranging another meeting with Zed. But Neve had already made up her mind that she didn't want to. It would be pushing things too much, and Neve was not a pushy person. Besides, Zed was *her* friend, not Holly's. Perhaps this was selfish but she could not help it. Zed had become a part of her personal life, not just because his mother had married her father but also because of what had been said in her father's study.

On Wednesday her father phoned. 'That was a really nice thing to do,' he said, meaning the trip to Covent Garden. 'Zed really enjoyed himself.'

'Good,' Neve said. She was glad that her father had realised she had made an effort, but she did not want him dwelling on it.

'I thought you might like to come round on Friday evening to see Zed off,' he said, 'since you two seem to be getting on now.'

She thought about saying to him, 'Only if you promise not to start talking about things from my childhood,' but she did not. She had still not entirely forgiven him. But she agreed to come round at about six o'clock. He sounded pleased with himself. He probably thought he was doing a great job in bringing everybody together.

In fact Zed's last evening was not at all what she had expected. It was Yvonne who opened the door when she arrived. She kissed Neve on both cheeks 'How lovely to see you,' she said. Neve doubted whether she really thought this. Their relationship was always going to be difficult. At least that was how she saw it. Still she remembered what her mother had said about being positive. Yvonne was making an effort. She ought to do the same. She made her way into the kitchen where food of all kinds was spread out on plates and bowls on the table. 'This looks good,' she said.

'Yvonne did most of it,' Laurence told her. He sounded proud, as though Yvonne had just been awarded a swimming certificate. Neve sighed. She supposed that was what it was like when people of her father's age fell in love. Each one thought the other was marvellous and went around spreading the news.

When she had loaded up her plate with food, she went along the hall and into the front room. Zed was sitting on the sofa with a plate on his lap. He smiled when he saw her. 'I'm glad you could come,' he said.

'Thank you,' Neve said. It was so strange, this relationship. It was hard to know how to behave and what to say.

They both sat down and concentrated on eating for a while. Zed seemed to be having trouble eating from a plate on his lap. 'I'm not really used to this,' he said.

'Do you always have meals at a table?' Neve asked.

'Usually. My father is a very conventional man. And my mother, too, normally. I think she's making a effort to be more relaxed because of you.'

'Because of me?'

'She wants you to feel at home here.'

'I see.'

'I thought you might have brought your friend, Holly,' he went on.

She felt a little disappointed to hear him say that. 'Maybe I should have asked her.'

'I'm glad you didn't,' he said. 'I like her but it's easier like this. Holly is nice but she's a bit...' He struggled to find the right word. 'A bit too much? Do you know what I mean?'

'Yes.' And that was Holly dealt with. She liked that about Zed. He spoke his mind. They talked about the day they had spent in Covent Garden. Zed said that he was planning to live in London when he left school. He was going to take a year out before going to university. She asked him what he wanted to study. He shrugged. 'Engineering maybe. I'm not sure.' He asked Neve if she wanted to be a journalist.

'Why should I want to be a journalist?' she replied.

'Just because my father is one?'

Zed shrugged. 'Things run in families sometimes. You're just very like him, that's all.'

'I'm not at all like my father,' Neve said.

Zed made a gesture with his right hand that she felt could mean anything and nothing.

'What's that supposed to mean?'

'I think you may be more like him than you realise.'

Neve was beginning to feel cross with him now. 'I'm not one bit like him,' she said. 'I'm reliable, dependable, I keep my promises and I don't want to spend all my time in the limelight.'

Zed looked puzzled. 'In the limelight?' he said.

'It's a phrase,' she told him. 'It means the centre of attention.'

'In the limelight,' Zed repeated, as if he was filing the phrase away for future reference. Then he returned his attention to what Neve had just said. 'No,' he agreed, 'you are not interested in being in the limelight. But I still think you are like your father, in a way.'

Before Neve could protest any further, Yvonne came into the room carrying a plate of food. She sat down on the sofa opposite them. 'It was so nice of you to invite Zed to see Covent Garden,' she told Neve.

'It wasn't that nice of me,' Neve admitted. She was getting a bit embarrassed by all these congratulations.

'Well I think Zed had a really good time, didn't you Zed?'

'Yes, I did,' Zed agreed. He looked embarrassed, too, to have his mother treat him as if he was a little boy.

'This is lovely food,' Neve said. It was true. The food was delicious.

'Thank you,' Yvonne replied. She looked delighted at the compliment and seemed to relax visibly. She began talking about a market in Cambridge which she had enjoyed visiting when she was Neve's age. 'I'm sure it was not as exciting as Covent Garden,' she said, 'but I loved it.'

'I thought you grew up in France.'

Yvonne shook her head. 'I grew up in England,' she said. 'I got a job in France not long after I left university and I ended up staying for nearly twenty years. Of course I used to go back and forth to England a great deal at first but then, after a few years I settled. She carried on talking about the differences between France and England until the sound of Daniel crying interrupted her. Then she got up and disappeared out of the room.

'My mother and father are such opposites,' Zed announced.

Neve looked at him, waiting for him to explain what he meant.

'She is happiest when she is with people, talking, like she was just now. He likes it best when he is alone on the side of a mountain.'

'No wonder they got divorced,' Neve said. Immediately she wished she had not said that. It sounded so brutal.

But Zed did not seem offended. 'Sometimes opposites attract,' he said. 'But perhaps my parents were too far apart to start with.' He shrugged. 'I think some people are made for each other and others are not.'

Yvonne came back into the room then with Daniel in her arms. Laurence followed closely behind her. He was carrying a plate piled high with food.

'Couldn't you have got a bit more food on there, Dad?' Neve said, jokingly.

'He needs to build his strength up. He's been doing battle with Zed.' Yvonne said.

Neve looked at Zed.

'Your father and I have been playing chess,' he told her.

Laurence had always liked playing chess. He had tried to interest her in it when she was younger but although she knew how to play, it did not hold the fascination for her that it clearly did for him. 'Who won?' Neve asked.

'It's one game each,' Zed told her. 'We'll have to wait until the next visit for the decider.'

'I don't understand what you two see in it,' Yvonne said. 'They sat here until three o'clock last night,' she told Neve, 'not saying a word, just staring at the board. I went to bed and left them to it.'

'It's a wonderful game,' Laurence said. 'Every move you make has its own consequence. And the same is true for your opponent. You can't afford to ignore any thing that happens.'

The evening passed surprisingly easily, and without any unpleasantness. Only Laurence did not seem to be really enjoying himself. He was not his usual talkative self. As it got later he grew increasingly subdued and kept leaving the room to make phone calls. He came back each time looking distinctly unhappy.

When the time came for Zed to leave, Laurence, who was supposed to be driving him to the station, had disappeared again. 'He's in his study, I expect,' Yvonne said. She stood at the bottom of the stairs and called Laurence's name.

He came down the stairs frowning. 'I can't get through to Charles Steiner,' he said. 'I don't know what's happened to him. He said he was definitely going to ring me this afternoon.'

'Perhaps he rang while you were out.'

Laurence shook his head. 'The answerphone was on,' he said. He looked irritated. 'I've tried his office, his home number and his mobile. I've sent him three separate e-mails.'

'What about his friends?' Yvonne asked.

'Charles doesn't have time for friends.'

'Maybe he's travelling somewhere and he's switched his mobile off,' she suggested.

Laurence still looked unhappy. 'I really need to speak to him tonight and he knows that.' He looked at his watch, then he turned to Zed. 'Look, would you mind if I called in at the office on the way to the station. There's plenty of time and it should only take five minutes. He might have left a message with somebody there.'

'Of course I don't mind,' Zed told him. 'I can always make my own way to the station, if it isn't convenient to give me a lift.'

'No, no, that won't be necessary,' Laurence said. 'If we leave now there will be plenty of time to just call in at the office very quickly.'

'OK then,' Zed said. He turned to his mother. She came forward and put her arms around him. 'Have a safe journey,' she told him.

'I will.'

'And come back to visit us soon.'

'I will.'

He kissed her on both cheeks, then he turned to Neve, leaned forwards and, to her surprise, kissed her on both cheeks, also.

'Goodbye.' she said. 'See you again.' And that was it. He followed Laurence out of the room and a moment later the front door shut behind them.

'Are you sure you don't mind me calling in at the office?' Laurence said as they drove off.

'Not at all,' Zed told him.

'It's just essential that I get in contact with this man, tonight,' Laurence went on.

'Right.' Zed sat back and prepared to lose himself in his thoughts while Laurence threaded his way through the traffic. He began going over in his mind the events of the last few days.

But Laurence seemed to want to talk. 'The man I need to speak to, Charles Steiner, he's one of the most remarkable people you could meet.'

'In what way?'

'He's such a wonderful journalist. He leaves no stone unturned. Nothing puts him off once he gets started on something. He's like a terrier. He won't let go.'

'Is that what makes a good journalist then?' Zed asked him.

'Partly. Of course it's also the way he writes. He focuses so completely on the story and he always gets his facts right. If he's not sure about something, he doesn't put it in. So people respect what he says because they know he's not making something out of nothing.'

When his mother had first told Zed about Laurence she had brought a huge pile of articles cut out of newspapers and magazines and showed them to him. So he had known that her new boyfriend was a journalist but he had not realised at first how well-known he was or how seriously he took his work.

They pulled up outside Laurence's office. It was a large, featureless building, like a warehouse, with the name of the newspaper written over the entrance.

'Do you want to wait in the car, or in reception?' Laurence asked.

Zed shrugged. It didn't make much difference to him. 'In reception,' he said, after a moment.

The reception area was brightly lit. Chairs were ranged around low tables on which there were copies of that day's newspaper. Zed sat down on one of these while Laurence nodded to the young woman behind the desk, got into a lift and disappeared.

People came and went. Some of them clearly worked in the building. They walked straight through, nodding to the young woman behind the desk, just as Laurence had done. Others were visitors. They came up to the desk and signed a visitors' book. Then the receptionist phoned through to whoever they had come to see and within a few minutes someone stepped out of the lift to lead them into the depths of the building. The only exception to these two categories was a motorcycle courier who arrived with a package in a bulging brown envelope that had to be signed for by the receptionist. After that nothing happened for a long time. Above the receptionist's head a large clock showed the passing seconds. Zed tried not to watch it.

He had expected Laurence to be just a few minutes but more than a quarter of an hour went by before he stepped out of the lift again. Zed could see immediately that something was wrong. Laurence looked like a man in shock. He walked over to where Zed was sitting and stood there for a moment looking at him.

'Is everything all right?' Zed asked.

Very slowly Laurence shook his head. 'No,' he said. 'Everything isn't all right.' He sat down next to Zed. 'I've just had some very bad news.'

Zed waited for him to carry on.

'I'm sorry,' Laurence said. He made a visible effort to pull himself together.

'What's the matter?' Zed asked. He was beginning to get frightened. He suddenly had the idea that the bad news might have something to do with his mother, but then he dismissed that idea. Whatever was wrong must be connected with Laurence's work.'

'Charles Steiner, the man I wanted to speak to, he's dead,' Laurence said. He spoke as if he could hardly believe what he was saying.

'What?'

'He was found in his car about an hour ago.

Nobody seems to know the full details.'

'Did he have a heart attack or something?' Zed asked.

Laurence gave him that same, distant, dazed look, as if he was trying to remember who he was talking to. 'No,' he said. 'It wasn't that.' Then he made an effort to pull himself together. ' Look, I'm sorry, we'd better get moving if you're going to catch your train,' he said, but he made no effort to move. Instead, he continued to sit there, staring into space.

'How did he die?' Zed asked. It was clear that Laurence was unable to just get up and carry on as normal and Zed was beginning to get a distinct feeling that there was more to this than Laurence had told him.

Laurence looked him right in the eye. The dazed look disappeared. He seemed to be focusing properly for the first time since he had stepped out of the lift. 'He was shot,' he said.

Those three words changed everything. The chairs on which they were sitting, the table in front of them, the grey steel doors of the lift, the reception desk and the receptionist who was still busy writing up some kind of record - all these things were tinged with menace in a way that they had not been before. It was as if something nasty had leaked into the everyday world, staining whatever it touched.

'Who shot him?' Zed asked.

Laurence shrugged. 'I don't know,' he said. 'I can't find out anything. He doesn't have any real family and the Swiss police aren't revealing any information at this stage.'

'The Swiss police?'

'He was based in Geneva.'

'But why would somebody want to kill him?'

'Plenty of reasons.' Laurence shrugged. 'When you lift up a stone, you shouldn't be surprised if something nasty crawls out. He always used to say that. But I shouldn't really talk about it.'

Zed was not going to be put off that easily. 'Has this got something to do with what you were working on?' he asked. 'Is that why he was murdered?'

Laurence shrugged. 'I honestly don't know,' he said. 'All I know is that the organisation that Charles was investigating doesn't care what it does. They steal from the poorest people on earth.' He shook his head as if he was still too shocked to take everything in.

'You said that you were working on this investigation together?' Zed asked.

'Yes.'

'So if he's been murdered, what about you?'

'I don't know,' Laurence said. 'Charles was the one who had all the information. He had worked out nearly everything. He was just looking for the last few pieces in the jigsaw. That was what I wanted to talk to him about tonight.'

'Did he tell you everything he knew?'

'Almost everything.'

'So do you think they'll come after you?'

'I doubt it,' Laurence said, but he sounded as if he was trying to reassure himself as well as Zed. Suddenly he stood up. 'We'd better get a move on,' he said. 'You're going to miss your train at this rate.'

'I can get a cab,' Zed said. 'You've got enough to think about without taking me to the station.' He was perfectly capable of making his own way to the station, even though he was in a foreign city. If there was one thing he was proud of it was his ability to cope.

'No, no,' Laurence said. 'I told your mother I would take you to the station and that's what I'm going to do. Come on.'

Zed stood up and followed him out through the glass doors back on to the street.

CHAPTER FOUR

One day they were sailing over the seas in Balloon House when they saw below them an island which did not appear on any map. The Great Magician ordered Balloon House to land and they set out to explore. Soon they had made their way to the palace where the king of the unknown island lived. He was most surprised to see them but he treated them nobly and ordered a huge open-air banquet to be held in their honour. While they ate, he asked them how they had arrived. When the Great Magician told him that they had come in a magical house that could fly through the air, the king's eyes narrowed with greed. 'Seize him!' he said. A hand was clapped over the Great Magician's mouth before he had time to utter a single word and a sword was pointed at his throat. Then the king turned to face Alissa.

After Laurence and Zed had left, Yvonne announced that she was going to give Daniel his bath and put him to sleep. 'If you want to watch TV or listen to music, please feel free,' she said.

'OK.' It had been a nice evening, Neve decided and a lot of the credit for that was due to Yvonne. She had made a real effort to be friendly. From now on she should try to be nicer in return. She picked up the remote control and flicked through the TV channels. There wasn't much on. She was just getting vaguely interested in a programme about elephants when the doorbell rang. 'Neve could you get that?' Yvonne called down. 'I've got my hands full.'

The doorbell rang again as she stepped out into the hall. 'All right,' she called out, wondering who it could be that was so impatient. 'I'm coming.' Perhaps Laurence and Zed had forgotten something. She unlocked the door and pulled it towards her. In a fraction of a second Neve saw two men. They were wearing balaclavas over their faces. The next instant she was flying back into the hall as one of the men pushed the door hard with his shoulder. She cried out as the two men stepped into the hall and slammed the door behind them.

Neve's mind was racing as she struggled to make sense of what was going on. She wanted to say something, to ask these men who they were and what they thought they were doing, to shout at them to get out of the house, or to call out for Yvonne, but she couldn't speak. The men were carrying guns, she realised, and that knowledge was like a huge weight pressing down on top of her.

One of the men was short and heavy. The other was tall and moved quickly. The short man pointed his gun directly at her. 'Stay still,' he ordered. He spoke with an accent that Neve did not recognise. While he was speaking, the other man pushed open the door to the sitting room and went inside. A few seconds later he came out again. He pushed past Neve and went into the dining room and then the kitchen. Neve realised that he was searching for something or someone.

Yvonne appeared at the top of the stairs. She was carrying Daniel. 'What's happening?' she called. The short man looked up at her. 'Come downstairs!' he shouted.

Yvonne stood there, trying to take it all in.

'I said come downstairs!' he repeated. Yvonne began to walk down the stairs one step at a time.

'Hurry up!'

The other man came out of the kitchen and leapt up the stairs towards her. Yvonne cowered against the wall but he just pushed straight past and began searching the rooms upstairs.

Yvonne stood where she had stopped. She was still pressed against the wall but she managed to speak. Neve had to admire her for that. She couldn't have uttered a single word, herself. 'You can have all the money in the house,' she said. 'I'll show you where it is.'

'Shut up!' the short man told her, 'and get down here.' He spoke as if he did not recognise her as a fellow human being.

Yvonne came down the stairs and stood in the hall beside Neve. She was clutching Daniel against her chest, trying to shield him from the gunmen. He was making whimpering noises as if he could tell that something was wrong. The three of them stood and waited. They could hear the man going through the rooms upstairs. Then he came back downstairs and shook his head.

The short man, who Neve thought might be the one in charge, ordered them into the front room. Then he pointed his gun at Yvonne. 'Where is he?' he demanded.

'I don't know what you mean,' Yvonne told him.

A flash of anger showed in the eyes that stared out

at her from behind the balaclava. For a moment Neve thought he was going to hit her, but he didn't. 'You know who I'm talking about,' he said. 'Laurence Cunningham.'

'He's gone out,' Yvonne told him.

'Out where?'

There was a moment's awful silence while Yvonne struggled to think of an answer. Then the telephone rang. It sounded incredibly loud and they all stood still and listened. It rang four times and stopped as the answering machine came on. There was a pause, the machine bleeped and then they heard Laurence's voice.

'Hello. It's Laurence here. I don't know where you've all disappeared to. Oh I suppose maybe it's Daniel's bath time. Anyway, look, I'm going to be back a little bit later than I said. I got held up at the office. I've had a bit of bad news. I'll tell you about it when I get home. It means that Zed will have to get the next train back, I'm afraid. But don't worry, he's going to phone his father and tell him. I'll call back just to let you know that he's safely on the train. OK. Bye then.'

As soon as the voice stopped, it was as if they had all been released from a spell. The short man crossed the room quickly and turned the answerphone off. He ordered them to sit down on the sofa while his colleague went over to the window, closed the curtains and switched on the lights. He looked at Yvonne again. 'When he phones back, you answer,' he said.

Yvonne stared back at him as if he were crazy. She opened her mouth to say something but he did not wait to hear what she had to say. 'Just listen!' he ordered. 'You say exactly what I tell you to say and nothing else. Is that clear?'

Yvonne nodded slowly.

'If he asks where you were a moment ago you tell him you were upstairs with the baby, right?'

Yvonne nodded again.

'You keep your voice perfectly normal. You tell him everything is fine here. You ask him what time he'll be back and that's it. Try to warn him and you won't have a baby any more. Understand?'

At first Neve did not fully take in what the man was saying. She saw Yvonne's eyes widen with horror and heard her gasp. Then she understood. The man was threatening to kill Daniel.

'Do you understand what I'm telling you?' he demanded.

'Yes,' Yvonne whispered.

'You were upstairs with the baby. Everything's fine. What time will he be home? Got it?'

'I've got it.'

'Then repeat it.' He stood there, still pointing the gun at her, waiting to hear her say it.

'I was upstairs with the baby. Everything's fine.' That was as far as Yvonne could get. She started to sob.

'Stop it!' he shouted.

Yvonne took a deep breath and pulled herself together.

'Now tell me what you're going to say!' It was clear that nothing would prevent him from drilling his lesson home.

'I was upstairs with the baby. Everything's fine. What time will he be home?' Yvonne repeated.

'Good. Don't forget it! My friend here will be listening in on the other extension. Say anything else and you know what will happen.'

There was silence then, apart from the ticking of the grandfather clock which stood in a corner of the room and the noise of cars going by outside. Everything had become frozen in the face of the gunman's threat, the whole house was suspended in evil.

Daniel was clearly aware that something was wrong. He could sense his mother's fear. He began wriggling in Yvonne's arms. She clutched him more firmly to her but he squirmed and kicked. Yvonne stroked his back but there was an urgency about her movements that communicated itself to him. He began to make little moaning noises. Yvonne shushed him but her voice sounded angry instead of reassuring. Daniel's moaning became a stuttering cry.

'Make him shut up!' the man told her.

'I'm trying to,' Yvonne said but the harder she tried the more anxious Daniel became. She shifted him on to her shoulder and began rocking the top half of her body back and forth, stroking his back rhythmically. Daniel's cries only became louder. He squirmed in her arms, trying to turn his head round to get a look at the gunman.

'Please, Daniel,' Yvonne said. She was begging him to be quiet now but her voice had taken on the frightened whining tone of the baby's.

'What's the matter with him?' the man demanded.

'He's frightened!' Yvonne said. She was almost in tears but there was still a note of defiance in her voice.

'You're his mother. Sort it out!' He looked at her as

if he expected her to perform some sort of magic that would calm the baby down and switch off the crying like turning off a TV set.

Yvonne stared back at him while Daniel continued to struggle. Then she seemed to make a decision. She took him off her shoulder and lay him down on her lap. He was red in the face now, his eyes were shut and he had abandoned himself to wailing. To Neve's astonishment Yvonne began undoing the top button of her blouse. She was going to feed Daniel in front of the gunman. Of course it was the obvious thing to do. It was the one thing that might make him stop crying, but it seemed so impossible that Yvonne would let this monster with a gun see her do something so private. Yet that was exactly what she did do. She unbuttoned her blouse, then unfastened her bra. She turned Daniel to face her and placed his mouth against her breast. In a moment he had stopped crying and was sucking noisily.

Neve let out her breath, which she had been holding since Yvonne began to undo the first button. She turned towards the gunman, in whose direction she had not dared look until now. He showed no sign of any emotion. His eyes, which had seemed to grow larger with anger a few minutes earlier, had regained their former animal-like watchfulness.

Time passed in the room. Neve could not say whether a great deal of time went by or whether it was really only a matter of minutes before the telephone rang again. The man looked at Yvonne. 'Answer it!' he told her.

Yvonne stared back at him. The pupils of her eyes were dilated with fear but she made no move to pick up the phone. Instead she shrank back against the sofa. The man held up his gun and pointed the barrel to where Daniel was still sucking at her breast. 'Answer it!' he repeated.

The phone continued to clamour, seeming to become more urgent with every ring. Still Yvonne did not move. It was not that she had decided to disobey the gunman, she was simply paralysed. The threat to shoot Daniel had produced entirely the wrong effect. Her whole being was centred around her baby. She could not think beyond that.

'Let me answer,' Neve said.

The gunman looked at her in surprise. He hesitated. Then he nodded. 'Everything's fine here, remember.'

Neve took a deep breath, then she reached forward and picked up the telephone. 'Hello?' she said.

'Hello, Neve. It's me. I rang earlier but nobody answered.'

'We were upstairs with Daniel,' Neve told him. She was trying to make her voice sound as normal as possible but she knew that she must have sounded strange.

'I thought you might be,' Laurence said. 'Did you get my message?'

'Yes.'

'Are you all right?' Laurence asked. 'You sound a bit odd.'

Neve looked up at the gunman. She thought about telling her dad that there were men here with guns, that he should get the police, but she knew it was impossible. 'I'm fine,' she said. 'Everything's fine here.'

The man was pointing at his watch. He wanted her to ask Laurence what time he was coming back but Laurence volunteered the information. 'I'll be back in about an hour,' he said.

'OK.'

'Are you sure everything's all right?' Laurence went on. 'You sound a bit odd.'

'I'm fine,' Neve told him again. 'Everything's fine here.' If only there was some way she could make him understand what was happening without saying anything that would make the gunman suspicious.

'OK. Well, tell Yvonne not to worry, I'll make sure Zed gets on the train.'

He was getting ready to hang up. For the few short moments while she had been speaking to him she had felt as though a lifeline had been thrown from the outside world, but now the lifeline was being taken away again. In a moment he would put down the receiver at the other end and her chance to help them all would have vanished.

'See you later then,' he said.

'Meeonissibar.'

Immediately the receiver was snatched out of her hand and slammed down. 'What the hell did you just say?' the man demanded. He spat the words at her.

'Nothing.'

'Yes you did. At the end. You said something. What was it?'

'It's just our way of saying goodbye. It's a family thing. I always say it.' She could tell that the gunman was trying to decide whether or not she was speaking the truth. Just then the other man came back into the room. 'He'll be back in an hour,' he said.

The short man looked at him. 'Did he suspect anything?'

'I don't think so. He thought she sounded odd but that was all.'

'Are you sure?'

'Yeah.'

He made up his mind that Neve had been telling the truth. 'All right then. All we have to do is wait.'

Neve had hardly breathed at all while this exchange had been going on. Now that the men seemed to have decided to believe her, she let her breath out slowly, trying not to let her relief show. She had done her best. It had been utterly terrifying, the most frightening thing she had ever done, but she had managed it. The question now was: what would her father make of it?

'Is everything all right?' Zed asked.

They were standing in front of the Departures Board in the Eurostar terminal at Waterloo station. Zed had just been to a kiosk to buy a carton of orange juice and he had come back to find Laurence staring at his mobile phone.

'What?' Laurence looked blankly at him. 'I'm not sure.' He put the phone away.

'Was my mother worried about the delay?'

Laurence shook his head.

'Everything's fine,' he said but the expression on his face seemed to contradict that. 'It's just...'

'Just what?'

'Nothing.'

'Tell me,' Zed was certain now that something else had gone wrong.

'You wouldn't understand.'

'People are always telling me that,' Zed said, 'but I'm smarter than I look.'

It was meant to be a joke but Laurence did not smile. 'I don't mean you're not clever enough to understand,' Laurence said. 'It's just a bit complicated. Anyway it may be nothing.'

'Is it to do with my mother?' Zed asked. He was determined to find out the truth.

'No.'

'But you just spoke to her on your mobile.'

'No I didn't. I spoke to Neve.'

'What did she say?'

'Well nothing really, just this word at the very end.'

'What word?'

'Meeonissibar.'

'Sorry?' Zed was proud of his English. His mother

had often told him that he spoke better English than a lot of people who lived all their lives in England. He suspected that was just the sort of thing that mothers said. All the same he did not often encounter words he completely failed to recognise.

'It's a made-up word,' Laurence told him.

'Oh I see.' Actually he was not sure that he did see.

'It's part of a story that I used to tell her when she was a little girl.'

This sounded familiar. 'Balloon House?' Zed asked.

Laurence looked at him in complete surprise. 'Did she tell you about it?'

'Yes. She said it was important to her.'

Laurence nodded slowly. 'It was,' he said. 'Did she tell you the whole story?'

'No.'

'It's not important, really. It's just that the word she said, "Meeonissibar", it's like a codeword. Only the girl in the story and her father know what it means.'

'And what does it mean?'

'Danger,' Laurence said. Then he shrugged. 'I may be making a big deal out of nothing,' he said.

Zed thought about this. 'I don't think so,' he said. 'Remember what you said about chess. Every move has its consequence. You can't afford to ignore anything that happens.'

Laurence nodded, as if Zed had said what was already in his mind. 'She did sound strange on the phone.'

'In what way strange?'

'I don't know how to describe it. I know she often gets angry with me, but that wasn't it. This time she sounded frightened.'

'Then I think we should definitely go back to the house and find out what's happening.'

Laurence nodded. 'You're right. That's what I'm going to do, just as soon as you've got on your train.'

Zed shook his head. 'I'm not getting the train. I'm coming back with you.'

'Oh now wait a minute!' Laurence protested. 'There's no need for you to do that.'

'My mother is in the house,' Zed reminded him.

Laurence thought about this. 'I doubt if there's anything to worry about really,' he said.

'Do you?' Zed looked him right in the eye. 'Tell me the truth.'

Laurence shrugged. 'I don't know,' he said. 'That's the truth.'

'Then I want to go back with you and see for

myself,' Zed told him.

They left the station and went back to the car which Laurence had parked in a side street. Laurence said nothing while they had been walking but when they were both sitting in the car, he began again. 'Maybe I'm just suffering from paranoia. Maybe we should go back to the station and you should get your train.'

Zed shook his head. 'You have to trust your instincts,' he said. 'My father told me that when he first took me climbing. He said, if you get a feeling that there might be something wrong, listen to that feeling, otherwise you could end up dead.'

'Your father sounds like a wise man,' Laurence said. 'OK. Let's go.' He put the key in the ignition and started the car up.

On the journey back Laurence lapsed back into silence. Zed found himself recalling the events of the past week with remarkable clarity. In particular his mind kept coming back to the painting in the National Gallery which Neve had been so fasci- nated by, the one that showed the girl who was about to be executed. Why had they both stood and looked at that particular painting? 'Do you believe people sometimes get a hint about what is going to happen to them?' he asked Laurence.

'A premonition, you mean?'

'Yes.'

'I don't know,' Laurence said. 'Possibly. Have you had some sort of premonition then?'

'I don't know. Maybe.'

'What does that mean?'

'Nothing. I'm just being silly.' It wouldn't help telling Laurence what he had been thinking. The only thing to do was to put it out of his mind and concentrate on the journey. The traffic seemed to be very much worse than it had been on the way out. Every light was stuck at red. Zed found himself trying to make them change by thinking green.

Nowadays he was not easily frightened. His father had taught him how to deal with fear when they had gone climbing together. 'It's always there,' that's what he had said, 'but you have to learn to control it. When you know that all your equipment is working and that everything has been set up properly, then you are in control.' But something like this – a journalist found dead, a frightened girl on the end of a telephone talking in some kind of code – that was not something that could be controlled. It was not something that he was even sure he understood. And so fear had the upper hand.

They turned into Laurence's street. The house was about halfway down. To Zed's surprise, however, Laurence did not stop as they drew level with it. He slowed down but carried on past the house.

'Why aren't you stopping?' Zed asked.

'I think I might park a little bit further up.'

Laurence found a parking space and pulled in against the kerb. He turned off the engine. 'It's just that the curtains were drawn,' he said, 'but Yvonne likes to sit in the front room with the curtains open and watch it get dark.'

'That's right,' Zed agreed, 'she does. But maybe tonight she didn't feel like that.'

Laurence shook his head. 'She made a joke about it only yesterday. She said that in England everyone is terrified that someone might see into their homes so they draw the curtains as soon as dusk arrives, like pulling up the drawbridge of a castle, whereas in France nobody minds if people see what the inside of their houses are like.'

'It's just what she would say,' Zed agreed. His mother was always comparing England and France.

Laurence sat there gripping the steering wheel. Then he seemed to make up his mind. 'You stay here,' he said. He opened the door of the car.

'What are you going to do?'

'I'm just going to have a look around.'

Zed shook his head. He hadn't missed his train home just to sit in the car and do nothing. 'I'm coming with you,' he said. He opened the door on his side and got out. Laurence did not object. He seemed to have accepted Zed as an equal now.

They both walked slowly towards the house. It was one of the strangest situations Zed had ever found himself in. They were both walking towards the unknown. Neither of them had any idea what to expect when they got to the house. Perhaps they would find everything as they left it, but perhaps they would not.

'We'll go in the side entrance,' Laurence said. The houses in this street had been built in pairs. Between each pair was a side passage, at the front of which was a wooden door. This was the entrance that Laurence meant. Making as little noise as possible, he opened the front gate, stepped through and held it open for Zed. They walked up the short path that led through the garden. With each step he took, Zed felt more certain that their progress was being observed. He was sure that at any moment the front door would spring open and someone – he did not know who – would be standing there. He could feel his heart beating very fast as they reached the steps that led to the front door. Then Laurence turned and made his way over to the side entrance. Zed followed, keeping close behind him.

The side door appeared to be locked, though Zed could not see any sign of the lock on the outside. Laurence stood on tiptoe and reached over the top of the door, feeling for a bolt on the other side. Zed felt terribly exposed as they stood there, like burglars trying to break into their own house. At last Laurence found the bolt and began working it free. 'I ought to have put a proper lock on this door,' he muttered as he struggled to free it. 'Still, good job I didn't, I suppose.' The bolt slid back. Laurence pushed the door open and they stepped into the narrow passage that ran down the side of the house. Zed closed the door behind him.

'Shall I lock it?' he whispered.

Laurence shook his head. 'Wouldn't want to trap ourselves,' he said.

That wasn't a pleasant thought. Zed left the door so that it could be opened easily.

Laurence walked tentatively forwards, then

turned to Zed. 'There's a window into the hall,' he whispered. 'I'm going to try and look through it.' He flattened himself against the wall and edged towards the window. There was something almost ridiculous about behaving like this and Zed found himself tempted to laugh. But Laurence did not look as if he was finding this funny. When he was quite close to the window he stopped and moved his head sideways to peer in. Then he looked back at Zed and shook his head. 'Nothing,' he said.

Zed moved forwards to join him. He glanced in through the window. It wasn't possible to see very much, just a small square of lit hallway in which nothing was moving.

'You stay here,' Laurence said. 'I'm going to have a look in the kitchen window now.' He made his way cautiously down the passage until he came to the kitchen window. Zed did not like being left on his own. He found himself wishing he was sitting safely on the train on the way back to Paris. But he was the one who had insisted on coming. He thought about the little speech his father always made before they started out on one of their climbing expeditions. 'Accidents can always happen. You can never be completely ready for them. But you can improve your chances, if you stay alert.'

Zed concentrated on staying alert. He looked back over his shoulder towards the wooden door at the end of the passage. Nothing had changed. He glanced in through the hall window again. With a shock he saw that there was a man coming along the hallway. He was wearing a mask. It was all that Zed could do to keep from calling out. He could see the man's eyes and a little bit of his face, not much more. Fortunately the man was looking directly ahead of him and had not noticed Zed. There was just time to jerk his head backwards out of the way. In the split second that Zed was looking directly at him, he had been convinced that the man was holding a gun. He had been holding it quite casually so that it pointed downwards but Zed was certain, nevertheless, that it was a gun.

It was hard not to panic but he knew that panic would not help. He looked towards Laurence. The man was walking down the hall in the direction of the kitchen. In a few seconds he would see Laurence who was standing with his face right up against the kitchen window trying to peer in. Zed made a hissing noise. Laurence turned round and looked at him. Zed pushed both his hands downwards in a sign that

Laurence should get out of sight. Laurence looked at him questioningly. Suddenly he understood and ducked down, only just in time. Then, keeping his head well below the window ledge, he shuffled over to where Zed was standing.

'What did you see?'

'A man with a gun.'

Zed saw Laurence's eyes open wide with fear. 'Are you sure?'

'Yes.'

Laurence was silent. Zed could see him struggling to keep control.

'What are we going to do?' Zed asked. 'We can't just stand here.'

Laurence made up his mind. 'We have to get out and call the police,' he said. 'Come on.' He pointed back up the passage to the wooden door.

'But we can't just leave,' Zed protested. He knew that what Laurence was saying made sense but he could not bear the idea of just walking away, leaving his mother and Neve at the mercy of some maniac with a gun. Besides he was not even sure he could move. He felt as if he were rooted to the spot, like someone in a dream to whom things happen that are completely beyond their control.

'This isn't something we can handle on our own,' Laurence said. He spoke firmly but Zed could hear the tension and the fear just below the surface of his voice. 'We have to get out of here. Go on!'

Zed began moving back the way they had come. Laurence followed. At the end of the passage he opened the wooden door and stood for a moment gazing back out at the street. Then he stepped forwards.

He was horribly aware that he could be seen by anyone looking out from behind the curtains of the front room. He ducked down and made his way quickly, almost on all fours, along the front of the window to the path that led down the middle of the garden. Then he carried on down the path towards the gate, crouched over, half-walking, half-running. It seemed like the longest journey of his entire life. At last he reached the gate with a little dash and was out. Laurence was right behind him.

'Keep going!' Laurence ordered.

They headed in the direction of the car. 'Who was that man?' Zed asked.

'I don't know,' Laurence replied.

'Was he the one who killed your friend in Geneva?'

'I think we have to assume that he's been sent by the same people at least.'

Zed stopped walking and grabbed Laurence by the arm. 'Do you think he's already killed them?' he asked.

'I don't know,' Laurence said. 'I doubt it. It's me he's after.'

Zed found it hard to understand how he could calmly say such a thing. But Laurence's manner had changed since Zed had told him about the gunman. The hesitation had vanished. Perhaps this was his way of dealing with the threat to his wife and children. He took out his mobile phone.

'Wait!' Zed cried. 'If you call the police, they'll turn up with sirens and flashing lights. He'll hear them. He might do anything.'

'I've worked with the police before,' Laurence said. 'They're not stupid. And I know who I need to talk to. It'll be all right.'

Zed nodded but he did not really believe what Laurence was telling him. Laurence was acting as if he was in control of the situation, but they both knew that he was not, that it might not be all right, that the man in the mask was a killer and that every second that passed was an invitation to murder.

*

If she ever got out of this alive, she was going to be a different person. That was what Neve was thinking. She was going to do what her mother was always telling her - focus on the positive things about people and not concentrate on their faults. She was not going to moan about anything or anyone ever again. She promised that, though exactly who she was making this promise to, she didn't know.

She had never been really frightened before today. She realised that now. Any fear that she had felt before was just a pale imitation of this. She was terrified for herself, for Yvonne, for Daniel and, most of all, for Laurence. He was the one they wanted to kill. Her only hope was that he had understood her telephone message, but that was a lot to hope for. He needed to have heard her properly, to have remembered what the word meant and to be prepared to take the warning seriously, not just dismiss it from his mind the moment he turned off his phone. It was the slimmest of chances. She felt like someone who has fallen down a deep hole and is looking up the shaft wondering whether anybody is going to throw a rope down.

She glanced at Yvonne who had not moved a

muscle since Neve had picked up the telephone. She was still breast feeding but now, as Neve watched, Daniel's lips released their grip on his mother's breast and his head rolled back in sleep. At that moment Neve felt that he looked incredibly beautiful, almost like a figure in one of the paintings she had looked at in the National Gallery. They had been full of images of mothers with pink-cheeked, fat-faced babies. Daniel was like one of these, a picture of innocence, completely unaware of the evil that surrounded him.

Yvonne adjusted her clothes. She moved like an automaton. She did not look at Daniel; she did not look at the gunman; she did not look at the buttons which her fingers inserted into the buttonholes of her blouse. Her eyes were glazed over.

Neve was worried about her. What she had done in feeding Daniel in front of the gunman had been brave. Neve had felt proud, as if she were the adult and Yvonne the child. But Yvonne's nerve had failed her when it came to answering the telephone. From the moment the man had threatened Daniel she seemed to have gone into a shell, trying to create a bubble of safety around her by ignoring everything else that was happening. She wished she could let

Yvonne know about the message she had sent to her father. Then they could both share the tiny glimmer of hope that Neve was nursing. But for the moment at least, there was no way that Neve could tell her. They were on their own together.

It seemed to Zed that the police were taking an incredibly long time to appear. He found it almost unbearable standing on the pavement, doing nothing but waiting while at any moment his mother or Neve or Daniel might be shot. Indeed they might already have been killed or be lying in a pool of blood, dying, while he and Laurence stood by the side of the road waiting for something to happen. He pushed this thought away. He had to believe that they were all right, that nothing very bad had happened to them yet.

He stared up and down the street looking for a police car. In both directions the road bent away from him and it was impossible to see anything beyond the turn. Every car that came round the bend Zed felt certain must be the police, but each time he was disappointed. After a while the flow of traffic began to dry up in both directions and everything seemed to grow very quiet.

'Maybe you had better phone again,' Zed said, 'and find out what's happening.'

'The detective I spoke to understands the situation completely,' Laurence said. 'I'm sure they'll be here very soon.'

'Why do you think it's taking them so long?'

Laurence shrugged. 'I don't know,' he said.

'Why don't they just send someone here right away? This is an emergency.' All the criticisms Zed had ever heard of the police seemed entirely justified. All they could do was give motorists speeding tickets. When it came to solving crimes or responding to an emergency, they were useless.

Just then a red car drove rapidly towards them from their right and came to a sudden halt beside them. The doors opened and two young men got out very quickly. They were both wearing jeans and leather jackets. One of them walked up to Laurence.

'Are you Mr Cunningham?' he asked.

'That's right.'

'OK, Mr Cunningham. I'm a police officer.' He took a wallet out of his pocket and showed them both his identification. Zed was surprised. He had expected to see uniformed officers.

'What we'd like you and your companion to do,'

the policeman continued, 'is to walk in that direction.' He pointed down the road away from the house. 'Just walk normally. Don't run. My colleague here will go with you. At the next junction you'll see a number of police vehicles.'

'What are you going to do about the gunman?' Zed asked him.

'I'm afraid I can't discuss that. Please just do as I say and you'll find a police inspector waiting to speak to you.' He spoke politely but authoritatively. It was obvious that he expected to be obeyed.

Laurence and Zed did as they were told. Together they turned and walked away from the house in the direction the policeman had indicated. The officer who accompanied them was younger than the one who had spoken. He was wearing a baseball cap and looked even less like a member of the policeforce than his colleague.

'Do you know what's happening?' Zed asked him.

'You'll have to discuss that with the inspector.' That was all he would say. They continued down the road in silence. Zed looked back over his shoulder and he could see that the first policeman was bent over the boot of his car, unloading something that could have been a rifle. Zed tried to look more carefully but the officer with the baseball cap touched him on the shoulder. 'Don't stop!' he said. Like his colleague, he spoke politely but in a tone that made it clear he, too, expected his orders to be carried out.

As they came round the bend, Zed saw that a police car was parked in the middle of the road, blocking it off. A motorcycle officer was diverting all the traffic away from them. Now he understood why everything had grown so quiet outside the house. The police had busy sealing off the area.

They were taken to a minibus beside which a uniformed officer was standing talking into his mobile phone. When he saw them coming he put the phone away. He looked them both up and down briefly, then turned to Laurence. 'Mr Cunningham?'

'That's right.'

'I'm Inspector Harrington. He turned to Zed. 'And you are?'

'Zed Mercier.'

The policeman nodded. 'OK. Perhaps we could just sit inside the minibus for a moment and talk.'

'What are you going to do?' Zed demanded.

'We are already doing a great deal,' Inspector Harrington told him, 'as you can see, but I think it would be better if we talked about it in the bus.'

Laurence put his hand on Zed's shoulder. 'Go on,' he said gently. Zed climbed into the minibus and the other two followed. The inspector addressed himself to Laurence. 'Now then, I've been briefed by my colleague but I'd like to hear your account of exactly what's happened.'

Zed's frustration was reaching boiling point. 'We're wasting time,' he burst out. 'Someone could be killed at any second and you want to sit here and talk.'

The inspector's manner did not change. He looked at Zed and spoke quietly and calmly. 'There are well established procedures for dealing with an incident of this kind,' he said, 'and we are putting them into action. As we sit here armed officers are taking up positions around the house. Other officers will shortly begin evacuating the houses nearby. In the meantime I need to find out as much as I possibly can.'

'But what are you actually going to *do*?' Zed demanded.

'We are going to try to resolve this situation as quickly as possible and without anyone getting hurt,' Inspector Harrington told him. 'Isn't that what you want?'

'Of course it is.'

'Good. Then you can help me by co-operating. OK?'

'OK,' Zed said, resignedly. He was still not happy but he could see that there was some sense in what the inspector was saying.

'So I want you both to tell me exactly what happened,' Inspector Harrington continued, 'starting with you Mr Cunningham.'

Laurence went through the events of the evening and the inspector listened without interrupting. When he got to the point where he had spoken to Neve on the telephone the inspector frowned. 'What was it, exactly, that your daughter said that made you suspicious?' he asked.

Laurence looked uncomfortable. 'It's a secret word we have in our family. It means that the speaker is in danger.'

Inspector Harrington looked doubtful.

'Every family has its own special words,' Laurence insisted.

'I suppose so,' Inspector Harrington said. He did not sound convinced. 'Did your daughter say anything else?'

'Not much. It was mostly me speaking. I asked if

she'd got my message and told her I'd be back in about an hour.'

'I see.' It was hard to tell what the inspector thought of Laurence's story. 'So you decided to drive home?'

'That's right,' Laurence described how they had parked further up the road, then crept along the passage at the side of the house and peered in through the windows. The inspector listened to all of this with the same grave attention but Zed felt increasingly sure that he did not believe a word of it.

'And it was you who saw the gunman?' he said, turning to Zed.

'That's right.'

'Could you describe him?'

'Not really. He was wearing a mask.'

'But you're sure he was carrying a gun?'

'Yes.'

'Right,' Inspector Harrington said. 'That will do for the present. I'd like you to stay in this minibus, out of the way.'

'Just a minute,' Laurence said. 'I'd like to know what you intend to do next. I think we're entitled to know that.'

Inspector Harrington nodded. 'Of course you are.

As I explained, we are following a set procedure. At the moment we're securing the area. Emergency services are on standby and we're expecting a trained police negotiator to arrive at any moment. When everything is in place, we shall make contact.'

'How will you do that?' Laurence asked.

'By telephone.'

'You mean you're going to phone up and ask to speak to the gunman?' Zed demanded incredulously.

'That's right,' Inspector Harrington said. 'Now if you don't mind, I've got a lot of things which need my attention.' He got up and went out of the minibus.

Zed turned to Laurence. 'I don't believe it!' he said. 'What kind of a plan is that?'

'It's probably the best thing to do,' Laurence replied.

Zed kicked the seat in front of him. 'It's a stupid thing to do. What if the gunman panics and starts shooting?'

'I've reported on situations like this,' Laurence said. 'The police know what they're doing.'

'So there's nothing we can do except wait?' Zed said, despairingly.

'Nothing,' Laurence said, 'except...' he broke off

and it seemed to Zed that his eyes lit up for the briefest of moments.

'Except what?' Zed demanded. He felt sure that Laurence was about to suggest something they could do, an idea that no one else had thought of. But if Laurence had entertained any such thought he seemed to dismiss it again equally quickly

'Except leave it to the police,' he said, shaking his head. 'That's all we can do: leave it to them and wait.'

There was a fly in one corner of the ceiling. For some reason Neve found herself watching it intently. It had hardly moved since she had first noticed it, except to clean its back legs, move forward a few centimetres and then stop again. It was early in the year for flies. Perhaps that was why this one was so listless. The summer was the season for insects, but summer seemed a long way away now.

The short gunman was watching them. The other man had gone out of the room. Neve tried to look anywhere but in his direction. But from time to time she could not help glancing at him. Whenever she did, he stared back at her fiercely. It must have been hot beneath that mask but he showed no sign of discomfort. He sat opposite still clutching his gun, which was pointed directly at Neve, watching and listening, his concentration never wavering for a moment. It was silent in the room, except for the sound of the clock ticking. Even the noise of the street outside seemed to have faded away, sucked into the vacuum of terror.

Suddenly Yvonne spoke. 'I want to use the bathroom,' she said. The abrupt interruption to the silence made Neve jump. They were the first words Yvonne had uttered since the telephone had rung and her voice was unrecognisable, quavering and cracked like an old woman's.

The man looked at her but he said nothing. It was as if she had not spoken.

'I want to use the bathroom,' Yvonne repeated, more firmly this time.

'Well you'll have to wait,' he said. He sounded bored and irritable, as if he were talking to a difficult child.

Yvonne stood up. 'I can't wait,' she said. She began to walk towards the door.

Neve saw a look of surprise come into the man's eyes. He got to his feet quickly. 'Just stay there,' he said, speaking each word slowly and clearly. Neve looked from him to Yvonne wondering what was going to happen. Yvonne had a wild look about her, like someone who might be capable of anything. Perhaps the gunman thought so too, because he stepped past her, opened the door and called out to his companion.

The other man came rapidly down the stairs and stood in the doorway looking into the room.

'She wants to use the bathroom,' his boss told him. 'Keep an eye on her.' He turned back to Yvonne. 'Go on then, but hurry up!'

Yvonne was still clutching Daniel to her breast. Neve looked at her. 'I can hold Daniel, if you like,' she said. She spoke as gently and as reassuringly as possible.

Yvonne turned in her direction but it was as if she did not recognise Neve or as if she suspected her of being on the side of the gunmen. When Neve put her hands out to take Daniel, Yvonne shook her head and drew back as if she had been burned.

'Get on with it!' the short man ordered.

Yvonne disappeared upstairs.

Neve was just beginning to think that Yvonne had been gone for rather a long time when she heard the man upstairs shouting something. Then he began hammering on the bathroom door.

The man downstairs looked uneasy. He glanced at Neve. 'Don't move!' he told her. Then he walked over to the doorway and shouted 'What's going on?'

'She won't come out.'

'Well make her!'

Neve heard the man upstairs call out, 'Come out or I'll shoot.' She heard Yvonne shout something. Then the sound of a gunshot tore the house apart.

CHAPTER FIVE

The moment Alissa spoke the Unfathomable Word the air grew strangely still. The king must have noticed it, for he looked all around him uncertainly as if he was not sure what he was looking for. 'What have you done?' he demanded, but Alissa could not answer. She looked over at her father and it seemed to her that The Great Magician's eyes were full of fear. She remembered his warning that the Unfathomable Word also brings death and destruction. Suddenly there was a huge flash of light and she closed her eyes.

They had been sitting in the minibus for about ten minutes with nothing to do except stare out of the windows and try to imagine what must be happening further up the road when Inspector Harrington reappeared.

'What's happening?' Laurence asked him.

Inspector Harrington sat down. 'We're continuing to follow the established procedures,' he replied.

'Procedures!' Zed said, scornfully. It seemed to be the inspector's answer to everything.

Inspector Harrington ignored his comment. 'I'd like to ask you some questions about the layout of the house,' he said to Laurence. He produced a neatly drawn diagram of the inside of the house. 'Is this correct?'

Laurence picked up the map and studied it carefully. 'I think so,' he said.

Just then a uniformed officer appeared in the doorway. He put his head inside. 'Excuse me, sir,' he said. 'There's been a development.' He handed the inspector a note.

'What's happened?' Laurence asked.

The inspector read the note. 'We've had a report of gunfire from inside the house,' he told them.

Zed felt as though someone was squeezing all the air out of his chest.

'I want my wife and children out of there,' Laurence said.

Inspector Harrington nodded. 'We all do, Mr Cunningham,' he said.

'So what are you going to do about it?'

'I'm afraid we're going to have to go in there and get them.'

The plan was straightforward. Inspector Harrington would go to the front door and ring the door bell. This would attract the gunman's attention while armed police would enter at the rear of the house. The whole operation would be co-ordinated by an officer with a mobile phone sitting in an unmarked car that had been parked opposite the house.

Zed was astonished at the simplicity of the tactics. 'But the gunman will shoot you,' he pointed out.

The inspector nodded. 'That's a possibility,' he agreed, 'but it's one I face every day. Now I really can't afford to waste any more time.' He got up to go.

'I don't think it's going to work,' Laurence said.

The inspector raised his eyebrows. 'With all due respect, Mr Cunningham,' he began.

But Laurence interrupted him. 'They know I should be back by now. They'll be looking out the window wondering where I've got to. As soon as they see a policeman approaching the house, somebody's going to get hurt.'

'I'm afraid there's always that chance,' Inspector Harrington told him.

'Let me go to the front door,' Laurence said.

It was the last thing Zed had expected to hear him say. He could see from the inspector's face that he was just as surprised. 'I'm afraid that's out of the question,' he said. 'You can help me most, both of you, by keeping out of the way.' With that he turned and climbed out of the minibus.

After he had gone, Zed and Laurence sat in silence. Like Laurence, Zed had no faith in the inspector's plan but there seemed to be no way forward. 'There must be something we can do,' he said to Laurence. 'Can't you think of anything?'

Laurence took out his mobile phone.

'Who are you going to call?' Zed asked eagerly.

'The officer I spoke to earlier,' Laurence replied. 'We've worked together in the past. He knows me.'

Zed struggled for a moment to think of the English phrase which described what Laurence was suggesting. 'Are you going to pull rank?' he said at last.

'I'm going to try,' Laurence told him.

'Get in there!' the gunman said angrily. He thrust Yvonne into the room in front of him. She was sobbing and still clutching Daniel who was crying loudly. 'Shut up!' he told her.

Yvonne struggled to control the violent sobs that racked her body.

'What the hell was that about?' the short man demanded, angrily.

'She wouldn't come out.'

'So you thought it was a good idea to start shooting?'

'It was a warning. She needed to know we were serious.' He sounded apologetic.

The short man looked at him with contempt. 'It was a stupid thing to do,' he said.

'She wouldn't come out!'

'So you decided to attract everyone's attention?'

The two men were facing each other. Although she could not see their faces because of their balaclavas, Neve knew that they were glaring at each other. A struggle for power was going on between the two of them, like two animals competing for supremacy. But the struggle did not last long.

The taller man backed down. 'She could have been using a phone,' he said. He sounded almost apologetic.

The other man dismissed this. 'From now on you do nothing unless I tell you. Now look out of the window and see what's happening.' He turned back to Yvonne. 'Sit down and make that baby be quiet.'

Yvonne did as she was told and, surprisingly perhaps, Daniel began to quieten down. His furious wailing grew less, then stopped altogether. The tension in the room dropped very slightly. It was possible to breathe regularly again.

'What's going on out there?' the short man demanded. 'What's happened to all the traffic?'

'There's somebody parked a little way up the road sitting in his car,' the other man said. 'He might be using a mobile phone. I can't tell from here.'

'Go upstairs and look.'

The taller man left the room. His boss sat down on a chair. He kept his eyes firmly fixed on them. It was hard to tell what he thought with that mask on, but Neve could sense that he was getting nervous.

Laurence put his phone away. 'He's going to see what he can do,' he told Zed. 'He'll talk to Harrington but operational decisions are taken by the officer in charge of the incident on the ground so it's Harrington's decision. He has to carry the can if anything goes wrong.'

Zed shook his head. 'No,' he said. 'We have to carry the can if anything goes wrong. You and me. It's our family.'

Laurence took a notebook and pen out of his pocket and began writing.

'What are you writing?' Zed asked him.

'It's not important,' Laurence said.

That was a strange answer, Zed thought. He looked to Zed as though he were writing down notes. Zed found it surprising that Laurence could not stop behaving like a journalist, even now, even when his family's lives were at stake. He turned away. He did not want to think about the gunshot. So all he could do was suspend his thoughts, try to block out everything, think about nothing.

A few minutes later Inspector Harrington reappeared. 'I've been asked to reconsider what you have to say,' he said, a little stiffly.

'Thank you,' Laurence said. He explained his plan in detail.

The inspector listened without interruption. Then he spoke. 'If we agree to this, you must understand that it would be entirely at your own risk,' he said.

Laurence opened his notebook and tore out the sheet of paper on which he had been writing. 'I've already made a written statement to that effect,' he said.

The inspector looked surprised. He took the piece of paper and read it carefully. Then he looked back at Laurence. 'You really want to do this, don't you?' he said.

'Yes.'

'But why?'

'Because I think it's our best chance.'

Inspector Harrington took a deep breath. He seemed to be weighing up the chances. At last he spoke. 'OK,' he said. 'We'll do it.'

The gunman looked directly at Neve. 'Where is he?' he demanded. 'Where is your famous father?'

He was definitely nervous, she decided. She stared back at him, not knowing what she should say, but it seemed that he did not expect an answer. He moved so that he was standing half in and half out of the doorway. 'What's happening?' he called up the stairs.

The other man came down again. 'There is someone using a phone,' he said.

'Watch them!' the short man told him. 'And I don't want any stupid behaviour this time - from anyone.' He glared at them all, then disappeared upstairs.

Neve felt even more frightened. This man was unpredictable. He had been looking hard at Yvonne.

Now he spoke. 'I should have killed you.'

Neve felt sure that he would like to kill them both right now, without any more discussion, just to get them out of the way so that he could concentrate on the job in hand. She sensed that he was not as patient as his colleague. That was why the short man was in charge. He made the decisions because he thought things out. This gunman was less clever but more dangerous. He might do anything.

She wondered about the man in the car who was using his phone. Was he just chatting to a friend or was he reporting the gunshot? Surely he must have heard it if he was within sight of the window? Or was it her father?

Time in the room seemed to have slowed down to the point where it had almost stopped. Neve was aware of every second that passed and every tiny thing that happened. She felt as if she could see the individual stitches on the gunman's clothes. She could smell his sweat, lying heavily in the air between them, stronger than the baby-smell of Daniel, stronger than Yvonne's flowery perfume. Suddenly he moved and Neve jumped. But it was only to rub his nose. He sniffed loudly. Everything about him was brutish.

As if he had read her mind the gunman looked hard at Neve. 'What are you looking at?' he demanded.

Neve could think of nothing to say that would not anger him more. He took a step closer. 'I said what are you looking at?'

He was full to the brim with anger. It would only take the tiniest spark to ignite that fury. She shook her head. 'Nothing,' she said. But he continued to tower over her, searching for some excuse to let out the violence that was inside him.

Just then there was a shout from upstairs. A moment later the short man had come back in the room. 'He's coming up the road,' he said.

Those were the words that Neve had been dreading. Beside her she could feel Yvonne stiffening with terror.

'Are you sure it's him?'

'Don't ask stupid questions,' his boss told him. 'Just keep them in here. Don't take your eyes off them for a second.' He went out of the room and shut the door behind him.

Neve felt as if she were falling from a very great height, plunging through the air like a stone. Her father had not understood her warning. He was going to walk up to the front door, ring the bell, wait for the door to be opened and when that happened he would be killed.

She had to do something to prevent it. She could not just sit there and wait for her father to be executed. The only thing she could do was scream, scream as loudly as she could. But she had to choose the right moment. She would only get one chance. She had to wait until he was within hearing distance.

She sat on the edge of the sofa, listening with total concentration, straining her ears for the sound of someone walking up to the door. The gunman, too, was listening. His gun was still pointing directly at Yvonne and Neve but his senses were trained like radar towards the world immediately outside. The whole room seemed to be humming like a spinning top, as if it was filled with some kind of electrical charge.

Then she heard something. She wasn't sure at first but now she heard it again, more clearly this time. It was definitely the sound of someone walking up the front path. Now was the time for her to act. She opened her mouth to scream but it was as though she were moving in slow-motion. It seemed to have become terribly hard to get her body to do what she wanted it to. She was so frightened - frightened of what she had to do, frightened of what would happen if she did not get it right - that every muscle of her body, her will itself, was held in a lock by that fear. The sound she wanted to make was frozen inside her. She could not force it out no matter how hard she tried.

The footsteps came right to the door and the doorbell rang, shattering the silence as totally as the gunshot had done earlier. At the same time the scream burst out of Neve, taking over her whole body. Her every sense was focused in that sound, as though she had become the scream itself. She saw the eyes of the gunman grow wide with astonishment but it did not stop her. Nothing could stop her now. She saw his body grow taut and she sensed him steadying the gun, getting ready to shoot her. Then came the noise that she had already heard once before, the sound of a gun being fired. Neve closed her eyes and waited for death to come.

When she opened them again the room seemed to be filled with people, shouting things at her. She could not understand what they were saying but it didn't matter because two of them grabbed her arms and pulled her to her feet as if she were a rag doll.

Their faces did not look at her as they bundled her out.

She was taken through the back door and into the side passage. They were running and it was hard to keep up. She felt so very tired. Her legs and arms were terribly weak and her head was swimming. She still could not make sense of what had happened.

They were out in the street now and an ambulance was coming towards them with its blue light flashing. It came to a halt and a man and a woman got out wearing fluorescent green jackets. One of the police officers let go of Neve's arm, went over and spoke to them. The man began opening the rear doors. The woman strode over to where Neve stood.

'It's all right dear. You're safe now,' she said.

'What happened?'

'The police got you out. It's OK.'

Neve became aware that another ambulance was pulling up alongside the first. More paramedics were getting out.

'Can you tell me your name?' the woman asked her.

Neve had to wrench her attention away from the other ambulance to concentrate on what the woman was asking her. Then she had to think for a moment before she realised what the question meant. 'Neve,' she said, slowly.

'OK Neve, can you walk all right?'

'Yes,' Neve said, though she was not even sure if it was true. She could feel her legs shaking and she felt certain that they might give way underneath her at any moment.

'That's good,' the woman continued. 'Now we're going to walk over to the ambulance and get inside. Do you think you can manage that?'

Neve nodded. The woman was talking to her as if she was a little child, but she was grateful. That was how she was feeling right now: small, vulnerable, uncertain what was happening. She was happy to let this woman take charge of her.

'Good girl,' the woman said. 'Now lean on me.' She put her arm around Neve and they began walking slowly towards the ambulance. More paramedics had got out of the other ambulance and gone into the house. Neve turned her head to watch them. As she did so she became conscious of a small dot of blackness in front of her and then another, and another. Now the dots were starting to join up. 'I think...' she said. 'I think I'm going to...' and then there was nothing but blackness.

The next thing Neve knew somebody was pushing a wheelchair underneath her. The two paramedics were holding on to her firmly and lowering her on to it.

'What happened?' she asked.

'You just passed out for a minute back there,' the woman told her. 'It's all right. It's the shock, you'll be all OK in a minute. Just try to keep your head down.'

Neve sat in the chair with her head between her knees. She had fainted she realised and now she felt horrible. She was shivering with cold and a terrible headache had started. It was as if there was a metal ball inside her head that rolled about alarmingly if she moved too suddenly. Somebody put a blanket over her shoulders and that felt a little better, but not much. 'We're just getting you something to drink,' the woman told her.

There was a question that Neve really wanted to ask but just at the moment she couldn't remember what it was. She had a feeling that it was really important but it was like a name or a telephone number that is on the tip of your tongue but then slips away and no matter how hard you try to remember it, you simply can't bring it to mind.

Somebody arrived with a glass of water. Neve sat

up and took it but her hand was shaking so much that she could not hold it properly.

'I'll help you,' the woman said.

With her help Neve raised the glass of water to her mouth. It was incredibly cold, numbing her mouth. It tasted as though it had just been taken from a stream that ran down the side of a mountain. She swallowed and felt the coldness go down her throat and then deep inside her. It made her shudder.

'That's good. Now just try another little sip.'

Neve had another sip. This time it was not quite so startling. She could feel things beginning to return to normal. Strength was coming back to her body. She had pins and needles in her arms and legs and her head was killing her, but otherwise she was beginning to feel better.

What was the question that she wanted to ask? Suddenly she remembered. 'Where are they?' she blurted out.

The woman put her hand on Neve's shoulder. 'Keep calm,' she said.

'I am calm,' Neve told her. 'I want to know what happened to the others, my father, Yvonne and Daniel. Are they all right?' She struggled to stand up but her legs were still wobbly.

'All right. I'll tell you what, if you'll just stay here for a moment I'll try to find out what I can about them,' the woman said. She left Neve with her male colleague and disappeared out of sight.

The woman seemed to be away a long time but at last she reappeared. 'A woman and a baby were taken out of the house along with you,' she said. 'They were suffering from shock. A man has also been brought out with a gunshot wound. I'm afraid they seem to think that it's your father.'

'Is he badly hurt?'

'I'm sorry but nobody seemed to know for certain. But he's been taken to hospital and he'll be properly treated there. There are doctors on standby.'

'I must see him,' Neve said. 'I must go to the hospital.'

'That's exactly where we're taking you,' the woman said.

They insisted on taking Neve into the hospital in the wheelchair. She felt like a fraud. 'I can walk,' she told the paramedics.

'Count yourself lucky then,' the woman said. 'You're getting a free ride.'

They wheeled her straight into the Accident and

Emergency department and took her to a curtained cubicle where a doctor was waiting for her. The doctor smiled brightly when she saw them.

'This is Neve,' the paramedic told her. 'She's one of the hostages. She had a bit of a blackout earlier on but she seems fine now.'

The doctor nodded her head. 'We'd better take a good look at you,' she announced.

'I want to know how my father is, first,' Neve said. She had made up her mind during the journey to the hospital that she was not doing anything else until they told her what condition her father was in.

The doctor looked surprised.

'Her father was brought in earlier with a gunshot wound,' the paramedic explained.

'I see,' the doctor said. 'We'll have to find out then, won't we?' She disappeared out of the cubicle.

Neve's headache had settled down now into a dull thumping ache. Her eyes felt tired and sore and she found she could not stop yawning. 'A good night's sleep, that's what you need,' the paramedic told her.

Neve nodded. It was quite true. She felt so tired that she could not even be bothered to reply. She sat in her wheelchair, her chin resting on her cupped hand, trying to stay awake while the doctor was gone.

There was nothing to look at, except white walls, a grey desk, a grey metal trolley with various pieces of medical equipment on it and a grey filing cabinet. At last the doctor came back. 'Your father is in surgery at the moment,' she told Neve. 'He was shot in the leg, apparently, so it's certainly not life-threatening. I've spoken to one of the doctors who's been dealing with him and I understand that there's been quite a lot of tissue damage but I think the bullet missed the bone.'

Neve felt a huge surge of relief. He had only been shot in the leg. But then it occurred to her that this might not be quite so straightforward as it sounded. 'He will be all right, won't he?' she asked. 'I mean he won't be paralysed or anything?'

The doctor shook her head. 'I haven't examined him,' she said, 'but I don't think you need to worry. By the sound of things he'll be fine.'

'Thank you,' Neve said. She sat back in the wheelchair and felt herself begin to relax for the first time in hours. Her world could begin to return to normal at last.

'So we'd better find out how *you* are,' the doctor continued.

Neve found herself smiling. It was strange letting

the muscles of her face soften like that and allowing herself to feel happy. It felt like a new experience. 'Don't worry about me,' she told the doctor. 'I'm fine, absolutely fine.'

A police constable was standing in the corridor outside the room talking to a nurse and laughing at something she had said. When he saw Inspector Harrington coming along with Zed close behind him he stood rapidly to attention.

'Everything all right, constable?' Inspector Harrington asked.

'Yes, sir.'

'Good.' He turned back to Zed. 'I'll wait out here then,' he said. 'I'll have a word with your mother afterwards.'

There was a small round window in the door, set at eye-level. Through this Zed could just catch a glimpse of a bed. There did not seem to be anyone lying on it. He pushed the door open and went inside.

Yvonne was sitting in an armchair next to the bed, looking exactly as she had done the last time he saw her. Her eyes were closed. Daniel was lying in a cot beside her. She opened her eyes when he came into the room and regarded him with astonishment. 'Cedric!' she exclaimed. 'What on earth are you doing here? I thought you'd gone home.'

Zed smiled. So she did not know the whole story. No one had told her. She did not realise that he was the one who had seen the gunman. He thought about telling her but decided to save it for later. 'Well you were wrong,' he said. 'I'm still here.'

She stood up and he walked over to her. They put their arms around each other and stayed like that for a long time. He had never really believed that she had been hurt, not in his heart, but from the moment they had been told about the gunshot he had known it was a possibility and he had been very frightened until Inspector Harrington had climbed into the minibus with the news that she was safe. Now, finally, he could see for himself.

At last they let go of each other. His mother sat down again and Zed perched on the bed. 'I don't know what I'm doing here,' she told him. 'They want to keep me in for observation but I'm perfectly all right. It was Laurence who got hurt.'

'He's going to be all right, though, isn't he?' Zed said. Inspector Harrington had already been in contact with the doctors who were treating Laurence.

He had seemed confident that his injuries were not that bad.

'That's what they tell me,' his mother said. 'We'll have to wait until he's out of surgery but the doctor I spoke to seemed optimistic.'

'Good.'

They were silent then, both of them. There was so much to say that it was hard to know where to start. In the silence Zed could clearly hear the sound of Daniel's breathing.

There was a knock on the door then and Inspector Harrington came into the room. 'Sorry to interrupt,' he said. 'I wondered if it would be possible to have a few words. It shouldn't take long.'

'Of course,' Yvonne said.

Zed got up, bent over his mother and kissed her. Then he went outside again, past the constable on duty, and stood in the corridor unsure what to do with himself. He decided to go and see if he could find a cup of decent coffee, though he did not think it was all that likely. As far as he was concerned coffee was one of the things that France was better at than England. Still, he decided that it was worth a try.

He had not gone far when he saw Neve coming along the corridor toward him. She gave him a huge smile. He found himself noticing, as he had done before, how her face was transformed when she smiled.

'Hi,' she said, when they drew level.

'Hi,' Zed replied. He did not know whether he should put his arms around her, give her a kiss or just stand there.

'I've just been talking to a policeman about you,' Neve told him.

'About me?' Zed was surprised.

'That's right. He told me you were the one who spotted the gunman. He said you were quite a hero.'

Zed shook his head. 'That's not true,' he said, 'You're the hero. You were the one who found a way to warn Laurence. That was really clever and very brave.'

Neve looked embarrassed. 'All right then,' she said. 'We're a couple of heroes. OK?'

Zed put out his hand. 'Let's shake on it,' he said. 'Congratulations, Neve.'

She took his hand and shook it. 'Congratulations, Zed,' she replied.

They said she could go home when she liked but she wanted to stay in the hospital until she had seen her father and discovered for herself what sort of condition he was in. After a while her mother turned up. Judith had known nothing about the incident at all until two policemen had arrived at her front door with the news that her daughter had been held hostage by armed men and was now recovering in hospital. Although they had assured her that Neve was uninjured, Judith had arrived at the hospital in tears and had been unable to do anything at first except hug Neve and weep. She was still firing questions at Neve and Zed, trying to piece the whole story together, when a nurse came over to them. 'Are you, Neve?' she asked.

'Yes.'

'Your father is asking for you.'

Neve followed the nurse down the corridor to the room where her father had been put. 'He's a bit sleepy,' the nurse told her, 'but he's very anxious to see you.'

Neve pushed open the door and stepped inside. Her father was lying on a bed in the middle of the room. There seemed to be tubes and wires coming out of his body, attached to a machine by his bedside. But his eyes were open and he smiled when he saw her.

She went over to the bed, bent down and kissed him. She was frightened to hug him in case she disturbed anything. He took her hands between his and squeezed them. 'Neve,' he said. 'I thought I might never see you again.'

'So did I,' she told him. 'I thought you'd been killed.'

'Well I wasn't,' he said, 'but only because of you. I don't know how you thought of it, but it was brilliant.'

'Thank you.'

He shook his head. 'I'm the one who should be thanking you for saving my life.'

'Well I think you should be more careful with it from now on,' she told him.

'Believe me, I will be,' he said, smiling. Then his face became serious again. 'There's something I wanted to say. I've been thinking about it ever since this all started.'

'What?'

'I wanted to say sorry for not turning up at the gallery.'

Neve almost laughed out loud. It seemed such a small thing after all that had happened. 'It doesn't matter,' she told him.

'Yes it does,' he said. 'And I'm sorry for all the other times, too. Do you forgive me?'

'Of course I do.'

'It's not going to happen again, I promise.'

She would have liked to believe him. It would have made everything so complete. But a voice at the back of her mind told her that people did not change just like that. Right now he was weak and vulnerable, like a child. The test of his resolve would come when he was back on his feet. 'We'll see,' she told him.

'I mean it,' he insisted.

'I know you do.'

After a little while he let go of her hands and she saw that he was falling asleep. She sat down in the chair beside the bed and closed her eyes. It was all over, that was what was important. Her father was safe. She was safe. Yvonne and Daniel were safe. Only a little while ago none of this had seemed possible. As waves of exhaustion washed over her, the hospital room melted away into the velvety darkness and it seemed as if she was no longer Neve, the hostage, the hero of the siege, but a little girl again caught up in the words of a story, drifting on the current of imagination, and looking down from a very great height on a world that had once been familiar but was now changed beyond all recognition.

When Alissa opened her eyes the king was lying dead on the ground. His guards had dropped their weapons and were cowering in terror. Balloon House itself was standing before them, though whether it had descended from the sky or simply appeared in an instant she could not say. She looked over at her father and he looked back at her. Then, without a word, they both walked through the front door and closed it behind them. Immediately Balloon House began to rise once more up into the air. Higher and higher it rose until when Alissa looked out of the window the king and his guards were no bigger than dots and the unknown island and the vast, grey sea that surrounded it on all sides seemed to her no bigger than a picture in a child's story book.

There are more
great Black Apples
to get your teeth into…

BRIAN KEANEY
Bitter Fruit

"I hate you!" she said.
That stopped him in his tracks. She waited for one
second, just to savour the look on his face. Now he
knew how it felt.

Rebecca's dad is such a pain. He's always
moaning, and one night Rebecca's really had
enough. She tells him she hates him. And these
are the last words she will ever say to him.
Grief at her father's death is mixed with terrible
guilt. While Rebecca is trying to cope with
these powerful emotions she discovers that her
father had a terrible secret, and suddenly life
seems unbearably complicated. But Rebecca
must learn to face tragedy and the truth.

"A gripping read that will have you in tears
from start to finish." *SUGAR*
Shortlisted for the Angus Award 1999

1 84121 005 6
£4.99

BRIAN KEANEY
Family Secrets

Kate had never met her grandmother. "She doesn't want to see us," said Kate's mother Anne.

Despite falling pregnant, Kate's mother had never married. The shame felt by Kate's grandmother had driven Anne away to London. Since then these two proud women hadn't spoken. Kate feels responsible for uprooting her mother and so she is determined to help rebuild the relationship between her mother and grandmother.

Now Anne and Kate are making the long journey back to the west coast of Ireland where Kate's grandmother is seriously ill in hospital. But what if her grandmother won't see them? How will Kate find the answers about Anne's past life in the remote west of Ireland?

1 84121 530 9
£4.99

BRIAN KEANEY
The Private Life of Georgia Brown

New girl Stephanie is popular, confident and stylish, and everyone likes her, including Georgia's best friend. Suddenly Georgia feels left out and lonely. In a desperate attempt to fit in again she does something bad...

But her drastic actions only land her in more trouble. Out of her depth and sinking fast, will Georgia come through for herself and do the right thing...before it's too late?

1 84121 528 7
£4.99

JENNY DAVIS
If Only I'd Known

Livvie and David fall in love the moment they meet. They're so happy together they feel they could conquer the world!

But when they try to befriend their mysterious new neighbours they discover that life isn't quite so simple. As they get closer to the reclusive Mrs Parker, Livvie and David find themselves uncovering some dark secrets. And things are about to turn dangerous...

1 84121 789 1
£4.99

JEAN URE
Just Sixteen

Priya was special and I wanted to be special for her.

Sam and his friends enjoy boasting about their successes with girls. But then Sam meets Priya and finds himself getting to know a girl he can really talk to, who he doesn't see as just a sex object or trophy. Of course he fancies her too, and Priya feels the same way about him. Making love feels right for both of them, but then Priya discovers she's pregnant...

Will their unborn baby bind them together or tear them apart?

1 84121 453 1
£4.99